KING OF THE LAKE

KING OF THE LAKE

AND OTHER STORIES

KIRA MARIE McCULLOUGH

WordCrafts Press

*I dedicate this book to my Heavenly Father,
whose love saved this wayward daughter,
and to St. Joseph,
whose prayers have guided my writing endeavors.
Finally, I dedicate this book to my earthly father, C.D. McCullough,
who always believed in me as a writer,
and who would be proud to hold this in his hands
if he were here.*

Contents

Foreword

Kira Marie McCullough has woven together a series of brilliantly crafted short stories that are like peering through a window into the soul of another, but you've been invited to do so. The opening story of a minister and the wife who will never be at peace with the expectations placed on her, is especially powerful when told through the eyes of a child. There's a familiar quietness in these tales, like the feeling you get when someone is about to share a deep secret with you. Each story exposes the often overlooked nuances of humanity in relationships, parenthood, childhood, love, euphoria, and the helpless feelings that arise when your ideals crumble like a house of cards in a hurricane. If words were a paintbrush, Kira would be a most sought after portrait artist. In "Secret Life" the description of the Walker Woman blurs the line between storycraft and poetry. In "Her Best Kiss" the description of each person's unique experience of a shared kiss is alarmingly and humorously divergent. With each character that each story introduced I found myself internally saying, "Tell me more." And here's something I found especially fascinating. Beyond simply enjoying the tales in *King of the Lake, and Other Stories*, I found myself looking more deeply at others around me as more than just people passing by. Good writing does that. It opens your eyes wider at the wonder in the world around you. Don't be surprised if this book doesn't have the same effect on you too.

~Bill Vanderbush
Best Selling Author of
Unveiled Horizon—Reflections on the Nature of God

SUPER DADS
THE POWER OF FATHERHOOD

Not every tale is true, but truth can be found in every tale. A Super Dad is strong enough to uproot a tree or wrestle an alligator to the ground. He walks his daughter down the aisle to give her away, then takes her back when her husband leaves her. A Super Dad believes in marriage and wears his wedding ring even when his wife removes hers.

Though these are stories of fiction, each comes from my heart, and the pathos and joy of my own unique experiences as a daughter of a father whom I loved and admired greatly, and miss daily.

KING OF THE LAKE

> *"A father's blessing gives his family strong roots."*
>
> ~Sirach 3:9

THE BEARDED MAN

> *"It is easier for a father to have children than for children to have a real father."*
>
> ~Pope John XXIII

HER BEST KISS

> *"To a father growing old nothing is dearer than a daughter."*
>
> ~Euripides

King of the Lake

You enter the Lake by the rocks, or not at all. There is no path to follow. Only a high cliff overlooking the water and a rocky battle-field between. The boulders are Kings overshadowing the smaller stones. They shoot up from the sandless shore in spiry-glory, silently greeting us in the solemnity of morning. Catching a foot between them could sprain an ankle. My father's strength—and the rubber soles of his good tennis shoes—kept us from stumbling.

My father would lead us down from the grassy rim, carrying me in the crook of his arm, guiding my mother gently with the other, and bearing the burden of the heavy, homemade raft slung by a rope, hanging behind his back. The escarpment sloped downward steeply, yielding to a shore of steely-gray and watery-white rocks tumbling endlessly, bowing low to the boulders scattered about. The battle to get to the water ended when we reached the curling tide, and my father flung the raft into the green waves.

We visited Erie every summer, beginning the year that I turned five. My father drove the blue Buick the 150 miles that seemed more like a million to a little girl like me, from our tiny town of Duane to Lakemore, on the margin of the Great Lake. My mother packed ham sandwiches and cold watermelon slices so we could eat lunch in the car while humming along the road, whizzing past the flat farmlands of Ohio.

My father wanted to settle us into our cabin with enough afternoon light leftover for a leisurely stroll to the Lake before sunset. *That is when the water is most beautiful,* said my father. Especially when you're sitting on a park bench on the high cliff above it, eating thin ropes of cherry-red licorice from a paper bag you bought at the five-and-dime, and holding hands with your wife. This is where he had first fallen in love with my mother, his bride, while sitting in the shadows of an August evening, overlooking Erie, and talking about the books they loved to read and the life they wanted to live.

However, it was duty, more than love, that drew my father back to Erie in the summertime. As the pastor of a small church in Duane, he was obligated to attend the Annual Conference, a regional gathering of ministers. Every summer, all of the ministers and their wives met in a large auditorium with the windows flung open, for it was an old building without air-conditioning. My father endured a sweltering week of preaching, singing, and arguing, while cooling himself with one of the handheld wooden fans donated by the local funeral parlor.

My father would often sneak away for an afternoon swim with my mother and me. There never was a sermon, he said, that could inspire him more than the Lake. There never was a problem, he said, that couldn't be solved by splashing in the cold waters of Erie. And there never were two people he loved to be with more than his bride, Maggie, and me, his daughter, Marabel.

If ever there were a Lake that could turn you into a mermaid, it would be Erie. If ever there were a father who could turn you into a Princess, it would be mine. He was King of the Lake and I, his freckled, five-year-old daughter, his Princess Marabel.

We would walk from the cabin to the water, down the steep hill, to the rolling stretch of stones and boulders along the shoreline. My father would place me upright on the beach and take the raft from his shoulders and toss it into the churning waves, holding fast to the ropes. Wading alongside it, he would lift me above the billows and set me in the middle of the rollicking raft. He pulled the homemade boat while I, sitting cross-legged in my demure blue shorts and baggy T-shirt, gripped the smooth edges tightly. At five, I could not swim. Still, he headed for deeper water.

The raft rose and fell rhythmically upon the gentle ripples that grew larger the further my father went. The combers pushed us sideways, and my father strained against the swelling tide, steering us towards the heart of the Lake. Before the smooth emerald hills of water lifted him from his feet, he would stop and plant them firmly on the bottom. Then, he would turn to me and open wide his arms.

"Jump, Princess Mar!"

His kingly command inspired me to stand. As I rose slowly, balancing on my chubby legs, the raft tilted forward and back, rising and descending with such force that I was pushed to the edge.

"Jump, Princess Mar!"

To hesitate would be folly. Should I fall off, then, like the whale that swallowed Jonah, the frigid water would swallow me whole. And so, I jumped with flailing, stubby limbs, my eyes wide open in my upturned, sunburned face, and mouth laughing, and in one brilliant burst of light, somewhere between the air and water I saw the flash of my reflection in my father's eyes—not of an awkward, overweight child—but of a Princess.

Each time, he never failed to capture me in his strong arms, lifting me above the billows, snatching me with lion-hearted courage from the darkness of drowning. My open mouth takes in the spray and splash that tastes of seaweed and fish. We cannot help but laugh together. The song of my father's full, round voice is the bold bass line to my childish soprano giggles.

For a moment, we bob up and down, going nowhere. He holds me close to his sun-warmed, bare chest until my shivering stops and the surf rolls sweetly and the black-beaked gulls swirl in the sky as if to say, *There's nothing to fear.* With my father's gentle push from behind, I scramble upon the raft to jump into his arms again and again, until mother calls us to the picnic blanket spread with sandwiches and fruit and cookies. We rush from the water to join her for a quiet lunch together, shaded beneath the large oak tree on the bluff above the Lake.

I looked forward to our trips every Summer to Lakemore, and the delightful predictability of jumping from the raft into my father's arms; of devouring the picnic lunch beneath the cool shade trees; of sitting on the park bench with my parents and watching the sunset as the Lake murmured, low and slow, like a sleepy old man.

Then I turned nine.

That is when my mother's past sins came back to haunt us. Before she had met my father, she roamed the bars downtown with friends, drinking and dancing until early morning. My father teased her, saying that he had been the one to rescue her from the debauched lifestyle, by wooing her with his prim and proper pastoral ways. Yet, my mother struggled to settle comfortably into the role of being a pastor's wife.

When parishioners dropped by for supper, instead of preparing a homecooked meal, she served TV dinners or frozen pizza, and although moderation was now her rule, nobody could miss the flagon of wine on the counter. Instead of wearing modest skirts and scarves, she wore figure-hugging orange and pink pantsuits with flashy, silver hoop earrings. She couldn't help laughing at bawdy jokes, or telling a nosy busybody to mind her own business. The old ladies in our church whispered that she was a backslidden woman. Others said that she was eternally lost.

The cruel gossip in the church began to change my mother. She slowly lost her resolve to lead the good life of a pastor's wife. She secluded herself in the bedroom during the day, leaving behind empty cans of beer. She sometimes disappeared with the car at night, returning drunk, and she claimed headaches and tiredness were the reason she went to church with us less. My father tried vigilantly to dispose of the empty bottles she left about. He discouraged gatherings in our home and all the while kept begging my mother to stay home after dark, to quit drinking.

My father urged me to keep this secret. I could see the strain of his duplicity, as he tried to make excuses and pretend before his congregation that nothing was wrong. My father, whose tanned and handsome face had once been lively and interested, turned peaked and pale and distracted. His appetite lessened so that his Sunday suits had to be taken in by a tailor. My mother had slid so far into the invisible darkness of her past sins that even my father could not save her.

For two years, my father and I went to Lakemore without my mother. While tugging the raft into the cold waters of Erie, he would sometimes look backwards longingly at the ridge as if expecting to see my mother there, calling us to lunch beneath the spreading oak tree.

Occasionally, wandering clouds in search of water would pitch their tents above us. Sweet powdery clouds would draw the Lake's bounty upwards, deceiving us into thinking that all was well—until they had become heavy with rain.

As the thunderheads grew dark, my father would rush me out of the Lake and encourage me to run with him to the top of the cliff. We would stand beneath the trees that held the memories of our picnics there and observe the sky changing.

My father understood storms. He knew the difference between beauty and danger. When there was nothing but wind blowing, and the dark clouds were on their way to somewhere else, he knew. Placing his hand comfortingly upon my shoulder he would say, "This, too, shall pass." And it did.

His sagacity about the weather was the kind of wisdom that he later lamented not having in his marriage.

My father preached a sermon about marriage, just before his own ended. I remember seeing him standing in the pulpit in his long, black robe, with bent shoulders and sad eyes, and I wondered if this would be the last time he ever spoke, for his voice came with fits and starts and stammering.

"Today, I want to talk about marriage," he said.

He looked down at his notes as if he had forgotten the next part. A hush fell over the congregation. A worried deacon crossed over the platform, bringing him a glass of water. He refused it, waving him away. After a long time, my father raised his head and fixed his eyes on me, sitting in the front pew alone. Perhaps he saw the reflection of the man his daughter believed him to be—King of the Lake, with legs as bronze pillars firmly rooted to the ground, and arms of steel outstretched.

His eyes remained focused upon me for a long time, until his courage returned and the song of his full round voice resumed.

"Divorce is easy. Marriage is difficult."

A shuddering and surprised gasp rolled through the congregation, with whisperings and rustlings. For the first time, my father ignored the people. He kept his eyes on me.

"Every child believes in the eternity of marriage." He paused. With greater force, he declared, *"Yes, every child believes in the permanence of marriage. It is their birthright."*

My father preached that day with the zeal of a martyr, as if he were proclaiming the ancient rule for marriage destined to guide a future generation, but too late for his.

The summer that I turned eleven, the threefold cord of love that had bound us together unraveled. My parents would choose the easy way.

It was a drowsy morning in July, and the hot breeze from the bedroom window had wakened me. I got out of bed and rushed downstairs for a breakfast of Pop-Tarts and cold milk. My mother stood at the kitchen sink looking out the window into the backyard. As usual, she still wore her bathrobe.

"Good morning," I said.

She didn't answer. Instead, she groped for the kitchen table, wobbling unsteadily until she sat down, shakily, in a chair.

"Are you okay?" I asked. I could tell that she had been drinking.

She didn't answer.

"Where's Dad?"

She exhaled slowly, eyes closed. "He's gone."

I opened a foil package of strawberry Pop-Tarts and plopped them into the toaster. "I hope he gets some milk at the store. We're almost out."

"He didn't go to the store."

"Oh?"

"It's over, Marabel."

"What do you mean?"

My mother leaned forward and put her elbows on the table and her head against her hands. I could not tell if she simply had a headache or if she was crying.

"Mom, what's happening?" I asked.

From across the kitchen, I stared at her in stunned silence.

"We're getting a divorce," she said.

"But I thought…I thought you loved each other…" I said in a tiny voice.

She looked up at me with eyes that seemed lost and distracted. "Sometimes," she said, " people fall out of love…"

A wave of grief swept through my body like a storm that beats upon the shore, scouring the land until nothing remains; every other emotion vanished in that moment. In the wake of pain, a strange feeling of nothingness took root in my heart, weakening me so that I had to fumble to the table and sit.

I remember my father saying once, that God's forgiveness is everlasting, but man's unforgiveness lasts longer. When my father announced the divorce to the elders at our church, they voted unanimously to remove him from the pulpit. They could not extend mercy. It was the small hospital in Lakemore that reached out to him, offering him a position as one of their chaplains. My mother took a job at Woolworth's. We stayed in Duane, separated from my father by 150 miles, in the house that he had left behind. Summer became fall, and I went to school as the child of divorce.

In the beginning, I could not forgive my father for leaving me without having said goodbye. The Christmas following their divorce, I visited him in Lakemore for the first time. It was brief and strained. I spent most of my days reading books and playing the radio in my bedroom, alone. I even took my meals upstairs to avoid him.

Finally, he asked, "Why won't you talk to me, Marabel?"

I was standing at the bottom of the stairs, holding a plate of macaroni and cheese, ready to go up.

"I dunno," I shrugged.

"Didn't you get my letter?"

"What letter?"

His eyebrows lifted in surprise.

"The letter I…."

His voice faded.

"I gave your…" his words drifted. " I wrote you a letter. It must have been lost in the mail."

I continued up the steps and into my room. We did not speak of the letter again during my Christmas visit.

The remainder of the school year, I stayed in Duane, refusing to visit my father. My mother and I lived together in an uneasy silence, with strange schedules that kept us apart. I went to school in the day, and she worked at Woolworth's in the evenings.

One morning, Gordon showed up in the kitchen, unexpectedly. Tall and skinny, he walked with a forward hunch, lazy and slow, even though he must have been at least a decade younger than my father. The first thing I noticed about him was his breath. Even mints and chewing gum couldn't mask the stench of tobacco, which hung about him like a smoky fog. The best thing about Gordon, my mom told me, was that he had a better job than my dad, and he made more money. That seemed hardly possible to me because after he moved in, mom and Gordon never seemed to have enough.

I noticed that the picture of my father disappeared from the living room wall. I had loved gazing at the soft-edged portrait of my father in ministerial robes with a gold-trimmed purple stole hung about his strong shoulders. I admired the angular lines of his firm jaw, the bright eyes, and the slightest tremble of a smile ready to break the seriousness of the moment.

Now, there was a montage of snapshots taped hastily to a piece of white cardboard that had been pinned in the place of my father. Polaroids of mom and Gordon riding a motorcycle through mountains, of mom and Gordon sitting by the campfire, of mom and Gordon drinking beer.

In June, they were married in our backyard. Gordon's biker friends and coworkers from the trucking company showed up. Also, Gordon's two boys, Kent and Sam, who were nine and eleven. Because of Gordon, my mother was awarded custody of me. A two-parent home with two incomes impressed the judge more than my father's meager wages as a chaplain.

After the ceremony, I walked up the hill to the patio, where a table had been set up with butter-cream cake and ginger-ale strawberry punch. Looking down at the bottom of the hill where the photographer was setting up for the wedding pictures, I saw my mother grasp the length of her dress in one hand and with the other, shoo Gordon's boys up the knoll towards the patio. They zig-zagged around her, laughing. Finally, in annoyance, my mom grabbed both boys by their sleeves and dragged them to where I stood.

"These are your brothers," she said. "Keep an eye on them, okay?"

As she trounced back down the hill in bouncing layers of white taffeta, to the flat part of the backyard where Gordon and the photographer were waiting, I took a paper plate and the knife. As I sliced a wedge of cake, Sam scooped some punch into a paper cup and handed it to Kent.

"Here," Kent said to me, with a disgusted face, "You can have it. I don't like strawberries."

"Thanks."

I put down my plate and sipped slowly, savoring the fizzy sweetness. As I opened my mouth to take a deeper draught, something sharp met my lips. I choked and gagged, spitting the punch on the pavement. At my feet, floating in a swirl of saliva and pink cream was a prickly, black, plastic spider. The boys laughed. Sam ripped open a package of rice and dumped it over my head. Then they ran down the hill, vanishing among the wedding guests. Soon, they reappeared, smiling and posing for the camera as if nothing had happened.

Every other weekend, Gordon's first wife dropped off Kent and Sam at our house. They ruled over Gordon and my mom, who believed they could do no wrong. When the boys were there, pillows went missing, shoes disappeared, toys were broken, and the best food—cookies, candy bars, ice-cream—was offered to them before me.

One weekend, when the boys weren't there, I brought up the letter. I was at the kitchen table, waiting for my mom to finish making pancakes.

"Dad told me he sent me a letter," I said. Her back was turned to me, her hands busy flipping the golden-brown circles of batter bubbling on the griddle. She whipped around to face me.

"What did he say, exactly?" she asked.

"It probably got lost in the mail."

"Good," she answered.

"What does that mean?"

"Nothing. Don't ever bring it up again, okay?"

I looked down to see our dachshund, Jimmy, prance proudly through the doggy door in the den. In his grinning mouth he clutched a plastic object. Wagging his tail, he plopped a chubby pink arm at my feet. It was the amputated limb of my favorite doll, missing since Kent and Sam's last visit. "Those boys!" I yelled. "They must have torn my doll to pieces! I bet they buried her all over the backyard...."

My mother whirled around from the stove.

"Don't go blaming those boys for what the dog did!" she hissed. She waved the spatula at me, emphasizing each word, spraying droplets of raw dough through the air. "That's what you get for leaving your doll lying around for Jimmy to get. Those boys wouldn't hurt a fly. They're your brothers!"

She spun back to the stove and plucked a plump sausage from the pan. Leaning over Jimmy, she waggled the meat in front of his nose.

"Wanna treat?" she cooed.

It was a Saturday in August when I received my father's letter. Usually, my mother gathered the mail before I could. Today, she was still in bed when the mailman arrived. I took the letter from the mailbox, hurrying up to my bedroom where I opened it. In his masculine, firm handwriting, I read these words from my father:

My dearest Marabel, please forgive me for not saying goodbye on the day that I left...

I grimaced. Why had he waited so long to tell me this, I wondered?

I still believe in marriage...I still love your mother.

My breath caught in my throat. The penciled words smudged beneath my tears. I read the letter to the end. Then, I carefully put it back in its envelope and hid it under my pillow. With a flashlight, I read the letter again in the middle of the night, wondering why he had waited so long to send it.

A few days later, I asked my mom if I could visit my father for an entire week. She and Gordon seemed especially happy for me to go. They drove me to his house and let me off at the sidewalk. Mom and Gordon did not like seeing my father. As they spun around in a U-turn of squealing tires and flying gravel, I slowly walked up to the front porch, carrying my suitcase.

The old screen door squeaked open, and from the dark coolness inside I could hear my father saying, "Come in, Marabel."

I skipped up the last three steps and flew into his waiting arms, sobbing.

"I got your letter," I said.

He held me close, stroking my hair. "I'm glad."

I looked up into his smiling face.

"We haven't been to the Lake in a long time," he said. "Would you like to go?"

I nodded.

We hastily changed our clothes and walked down the street. It was mid-August, and heat shimmered above the pavement. My father's rose bushes and the flowers in his garden were closed tight against the sun. Even the trees along the roadside seemed to fold in upon themselves. From a distance, we could see the Lake twinkling in the afternoon sun, its emerald beauty luring us to keep walking, to dare to go beyond the rocky battlefield between cliff and tide.

We tumbled down the cliff from the precipice above, expertly avoiding catching our shoes between the rocks, skimming past the boulders along the way. Where the water met the rocks, we waded into the shallows, heading for the heart of the Lake, until we were forced to swim, propelling our bodies into the deeper waters. When our feet could no longer touch the bottom, we treaded upon the rolling, green waves alongside the schools of fish skittering shyly just beneath the surface. When our arms and legs tired of keeping us aloft, we rolled over and floated on our backs, abandoning ourselves to the sky.

Gone was the old raft. Gone, too, were the demure blue swim shorts and baggy T-shirt that I had worn as a child. I donned a T-shirt, even baggier, to cover the new curves and bulges of my body. My father was too much of a gentleman to say anything. He must have noticed, though. At the end of the week, before mom and Gordon arrived to take me back to Duane, my father pressed a twenty-dollar bill into my hand.

"This is for you," he said. "For swimming clothes. Our secret, okay?"

A few days later, my mom took me to Woolworth's to shop for Gordon's Birthday present. While she picked through a bin of ash trays, I stared out the large front windows. Across the street, a mother and daughter, hand in hand, entered a boutique called Lisa's Duds. As they passed inside, I noticed the mannequin in the display window. She wore a shimmering, lime-green bikini that sparkled in the flashing rays of the mid-afternoon sun. I reached into my pocket and touched the edge of the twenty-dollar bill, neatly folded.

"Mom, can we go over there?" I asked, pointing to Lisa's Duds. Absorbed with a red ashtray, she turned it over to look at the price tag.

"No," she said.

Summer was rapidly fading, and soon swimsuits would no longer adorn mannequins. Shop windows would display woolen sweaters and corduroy pants. I would be destined to wear a baggy T-shirt to the Lake forever.

"I need a new swimsuit," I said. She picked up a mustard-yellow ash tray with fluted edges, heavy and bulky.

"No, you don't."

Looking at the underside of the gold ash tray, she muttered, "Good, on sale. Come on." She started for the checkout.

My mind flailed for the right words. I ran ahead of her, blocking her path. I pulled the cash from my pocket and held it in front of her face.

"Mom, I can buy it myself! See?"

She stared at the twenty-dollar bill as if it was the serpent itself, twisted cunningly around the tree of temptation. A blotchy red rash rose from her neck and spread across her cheeks.

"Where'd you get that?" she asked suspiciously.

My stubborn persistence evaporated. I felt like a helpless child, whimpering, unable to speak.

"Did your dad give it to you?" she asked.

I cast my eyes downward.

"I said, did your dad give it to you?"

This time, her voice had pitched up to a decibel that even the shoppers in the front of the store could hear. A few scowled at my mother, while others looked at me with pity.

Embarrassed, I nodded, staring at the floor, wishing it would open up and swallow me. I had betrayed my promise to keep a secret with my father.

She snatched the bill from my hand.

"This will buy an ash tray for Gordon's Birthday," she snapped, slapping the money on the counter. The lady at the cash register took the money, wrapped the gift, and handed my mother the change.

"Here," said my mom. "There's ten bucks leftover. Go get your swimsuit."

"You mean—"

"Get over there to Lisa's Duds before I change my mind."

I blasted through the open doors of Woolworth's, escaping into the downtown square, running across Main Street to Lisa's Duds. Inside was cool and dark. A rotating fan hummed on the counter, wafting the scent of Jasmine incense, while the transistor radio played love songs softly.

A smiling, middle-aged woman greeted me. She wore white capris and a flowered cotton shirt and a yellow bandana wrapped around her wispy gray-blonde hair.

"May I help you?" she asked.

I pointed to the bikini in the window. "May I try that on?"

She nodded, and quickly disappeared behind a door covered by two panels of pink and orange curtains separating the store from the back room. In a moment, she reappeared, carrying a hanger draped with the shimmering, lime-green swimsuit. She handed it to me.

"This looks to be your size," she said.

I rushed into the dressing room and locked the door. I quickly undressed and wriggled into the top half, clipping the delicate clasps behind me and bringing up the dainty straps from the front to tie a bow at the nape of my neck. I wriggled into the bottom half, which comfortably hugged my thighs like a pair of demure shorts and snuggled against my hips. The waistband reached above my belly button, leaving only a swath of my stomach showing.

Usually, mirrors mocked me. My nose, which had grown faster than the rest of my face, appeared distorted, and my cat-eye glasses magnified the brown globes of my eyes, which seemed to bulge unnaturally. The flush of acne across my cheeks looked more like chicken pox than a sunburn.

But today, the mirror told me I was beautiful.

The graceful shirring of the material glimmered like iridescent seaweed against my tanned skin. The electric glow from the light above played with the fabric, making it appear to wave gently, like the elegant strands of seaweed below the Lake. Light and silky, the scalloped fabric modestly covered my chest. It was a royal bikini for a beloved princess.

Once again, I was Princess Mar.

My reverie was shattered by the sound of my mother's irritated voice. "Hurry up!" she yelled from the other side of the door.

I immediately put on my clothes and carried the bikini into the store where my mother stood at the counter impatiently drumming her fingers next to the bowl of Jasmine incense.

"Does it fit?" she asked.

"Yes."

"Good. It's fifty percent off."

I wore my royal bikini twice that summer to the City Pool. Then autumn came, and I packed it away in my dresser, eager for the warm weather to return so that I could wear it again.

The Summer of my thirteenth year marked the end of my childhood and the beginning of womanhood. My body had continued to change, and menstruation had begun.

It was a sunny day in early June when I pulled out my bikini for the first time in almost a year. I was hoping to sunbathe on the back patio for the afternoon. In the bathroom with the door locked, I struggled to wrap the top all the way around my larger chest. The clasps pinched my skin, and the dainty straps were strained to the point of breaking. I squeezed them between my fingers and tied a knot, hoping the straps would hold. I pulled up the bikini bottom, which seemed to have shrunk, revealing my belly button.

I firmly tucked in my sanitary belt, hiding the bulky pad as best I could. I felt anything but beautiful. The mockery of my nose, eyes, and acne had been cruelly launched at me by the reflection of the mirror. To hide the lower half of my body, I wrapped the beach towel around my waist, hoping that I could slip through the den unnoticed and into the backyard. Grabbing a paperback book and portable radio, I quietly tiptoed downstairs.

From the far end of the kitchen, I could see Gordon sitting in the easy chair in the den. There he was, mindlessly sipping a bottle of beer, which he called his *morning happy water.* He sat at an angle, facing the blaring television set, and couldn't see me coming from behind. I only had to take a few steps to his left, and I would be at the sliding glass doors. As I started to pass by, I heard a low whistle.

"Wow, Mar," he said. "Hold on a minute!"

I stopped and turned towards him, blushing. He looked me up and down, the bottle tipped halfway to his mouth, one eyebrow lifted, and his thin lips widened to show his teeth.

"Kent and Sam are coming over today. The boys are gonna drool when they see you in your bikini!"

I pivoted towards the doorway, threw open the flimsy screen and dashed out with such speed that my long, brown hair escaped its ribbon, flying free in the gusty breeze. On the patio at the bottom of the hill, I dropped to my knees, feeling unusually dizzy and nauseous, like the tail in a game of Crack the Whip.

I had forgotten that Kent and Sam were coming over for the weekend.

Here I was, trapped in the corner of two walls of the house, near the back basement door. The entryway into the boy's weekend cave. Thinking that I should give up on sunbathing, I tried the handle of the basement door. It was locked. I didn't want to pass through the screen to the den where Gordon sat. I decided to stay on the patio and sunbathe, hoping I could avoid the boys when they arrived.

Taking off my glasses, I placed them gently on the beach towel and stretched out on my belly. I rolled to my back a few minutes later, feeling the tingling sweat on my skin. Finally, when the sun's intensity caused bright white spots to dance behind my closed eyelids, and the heat made my skin pulse, I sat up. I put on my glasses and blinked. Just as I was getting to my feet, I heard the sharp squealing of the screen door opening by the den, and a *bang* as it slammed backwards. The boys were speeding down the hill.

"Hey, Four Eyes!" Kent screamed.

Where's Dork Girl?" yelled Sam.

At the grassy margin of the porch, Sam slid sideways until he was outstretched on his left side, like a baseball player tagging home base. Kent, red-faced and giggling, fell on his knees next to Sam.

"Foxy mama!" Sam whistled.

"She's hardly wearing nothin'!" Kent exclaimed, gawking at me with wide eyes and open mouth.

"Like a pin-up girl in a bikini!" laughed Sam.

"Yea, a Bikini Summer Pin-Up girl!" said Kent, with the same ogling eyes that I had seen on Gordon's face. For a moment, it seemed that they, too had passed from childhood into the world of grownups. But then they began their relentless, boyish teasing, proving that they were still too young to fully comprehend their own sensual natures.

Yanking tufts of grass from the yard, Kent stood up and pitched them at me until the air became thick with clusters of earth and roots and grass. I put my hands in front of my face to deflect the barrage.

"Stop it!" I yelled.

Sam got up and grabbed my towel. He whipped it in the air deftly, striking my legs, over and over.

"Hey, Goofball, take that," he snickered.

"Buzz off!" I screamed.

Tearing a branch from a nearby bush, Kent punched its sharp, broken tip into my bare belly, making red welts.

"Spazzin' idiots!" I shrieked.

I escaped up the narrow path between the row of Olive bushes on the south side of the house. Even with my adrenaline rush, I didn't have the speed and agility to outrun the boys. Their wild burst of energy drove them to inflict more boyish pranks from behind, as they chased me up the hill into the front yard, flipping the towel at the back of my legs and lobbing more dirt clods at my head.

As I rounded the corner, I tripped over the metal sprinkler and sprawled headlong into the grass. I crashed to my stomach, arms outstretched and legs still pumping up and down. In that instant, my glasses flew off. I rolled over quickly, but before I could get up, Kent had jumped on top of me, pinning me down with his knees and hands. None of us noticed that Mr. Darnek had come out on his front porch across the street, with a glass of lemonade.

"Say Uncle," Kent yelled.

"You win," I said, going limp.

"I win!" he yelled, letting go of my arms. Howling with triumph and clasping his hands together in a sign of victory, he leaned back, losing his balance. With a mighty shove of my knees, I pushed upwards, thrusting all of my weight against him. He tumbled over on his side, hugging his legs to his chin and crying in pain.

I jolted upright and jerked to my feet. Sam now frolicked around the yard with my cat-eye glasses stuck to his face, upside down. My beach towel swung back and forth in his hands as he swayed his hips with exaggeration.

"I'm Super Dork!" he scoffed.

I felt the fire of anger. A desire for justice had vanquished my embarrassment over my changing body and a too-tight bikini. My father might have called it righteous indignation. All I knew was that the boys had gone too far.

"Give me my glasses!" I demanded.

I stood with legs poised to lunge forward, my fists clenched in a gesture that made it clear to Sam that I was ready for a fight. He was shorter, and less muscular than Kent. Though I could subdue him easily, I didn't want to risk breaking my glasses.

He gawked at me, looking up and down at my bulges and curves, the way Gordon had. I took a step towards him.

"Give me my glasses!"

"Okay, okay," he said, holding up his hands. "Truce?"

Kent had recovered from the kick in his groin, and was silently stalking me from behind. Suddenly, with the ferocity of a boy with a wounded ego, he rushed at me. Sam tossed the beach towel over my head while Kent seized the corners of my bikini bottom. Beneath the towel, all was a hazy blur of green and blue cotton, but I could feel Kent's rough hands tearing the bikini from my hips to my feet.

The boys went into an uproar.

"Gag me with a spoon!" Sam shouted.

I tossed the towel off my head and saw him poking one finger in and out of his mouth, as he made retching noises. Kent had dropped to the ground, rolling in pretend agony.

"Golly!" he groaned, "that's really gross!"

From across the street, I heard a whistling from Mr. Darnek, who had stood up to get a better look. He had absentmindedly spilled the lemonade all over his pants. Everyone was looking between my legs.

Even though everything appeared blurry, I could see the thick white straps of the sanitary belt, still securely wrapped around my hips. The pad that had snuggly stretched between the clips had been ripped from one clip, and now swung freely from its elastic band. I could feel the soiled menstrual pad hanging between my legs.

Like devilish imps, the boys began to dance around me in a circle, Sam wearing my glasses upside down, and Kent, with the towel now folded between his legs and shuffling around in a parody of my predicament.

They began to chant, *"Bikini Summer Pin-Up Girl, bloody rags make me hurl!"*

Their laughter echoed through the neighborhood. Even Mr. Darnek guffawed from his front row seat across the street. I quickly yanked up my bikini bottom and ran to the front porch, fleeing through the door and up the stairs to the bathroom. Their voices continued from the yard,

"Bikini Summer Pin-Up Girl, bloody rags make me hurl!"

I turned on the faucet, rinsing the tears from my face, wincing at the tender sunburn across my cheeks and nose. I got into the shower and washed quickly in lukewarm water. I draped a large bath towel around my body, and crossed from the bathroom to my bedroom, shutting the door. I changed into clean clothes, and got into bed, sobbing until I drifted into an exhausted sleep.

I was awakened several hours later by a loud knocking on my door.

"Mar, it's time to eat! I made spaghetti."

It was my mom.

"I'm not hungry."

The door creaked open. My mom frowned at me, wrapped in a sheet on my bed.

"Are you sick?" she asked.

"No."

She folded her arms against her chest.

"The boys say you've been bothering them."

I rolled over with my back to her.

"It's the other way around," I muttered.

"What's that?"

"Nothing."

"Well, cut them some slack. They're your brothers."

She shut the door, leaving me in the dusky blue light of a summer's fading evening. Through the windows of my bedroom, I could see the translucence of the darkening sky, pink and orange at the horizon, with one bright star already shining near a hint of the moon. I thought sadly of the summer evenings like this one, sitting with my father and mother on the park bench overlooking the Lake.

Then, there wasn't anything to fear. Now, I lay stiff and tense on my bed, alert to the strange voices downstairs. From the kitchen below, I could hear the boys yelling at each other, fighting over the parmesan cheese. Eventually, Kent and Sam had their ears boxed by Gordon, because I could hear their hyperventilating howls. In a few minutes, they had stopped. I heard them thumping down the steps to the basement, with raucous laughter, descending the flight of stairs to watch TV until they fell asleep on the old couches.

As the moon waxed large and full, the contentious arguments between mom and Gordon began. His irritated voice drifted up the stairs from the kitchen.

"Hey, what are you doing?" he said. There was a shuffling noise and the sound of breaking glass. "Why'd you pour it all down the drain?"

"You drink too much, Gordon!"

Their voices rose and fell in crashing crescendos that dipped into disgruntled mumblings, incoherent and confused. When they tired of the debate, they clomped up the stairs to their bedroom at the other end of the hall, slamming the door behind them.

The house became quiet.

A cool breeze blew through the open windows, bringing the sweet scent of sun-warmed honeysuckle and freshly cut grass. The moon waxed yellow, dripping its light upon everything. The moon, like a gentleman, brushed the glowing paint upon the floor, careful to abide by the boundaries of the square windowpanes. Crickets lazily hummed.

I lay awake and imagined that I was five, again, and all was well on a summer's night. I yearned for the days of innocent childhood, of peace between my father and mother, the beautiful circle of three where nothing troubled my soul. Like a child catching moonbeams with her hands, I clutched the memories to my heart.

Drawn to the peaceful scene outside, I got up and went over to the wooden bench beneath my windows. I rested my elbows on the sill, breathing deeply the fragrance and feeling the pleasure of the solitude. That's when I saw him.

Mr. Darnek.

Under his muted porch light, I could see him, across the street. Like earlier in the day when he had come out with his glass of lemonade, he sat on an aluminum folding chair on the front veranda of his house, which was on a little hill overlooking the road. He could easily spy on the neighbors from his high perch.

His shadowy form shifted, as if he suddenly saw me, and was leaning forward to peer at me through the darkness. I heard a far-away thundering, like the night train, but it did not rise from the tracks near the river. The rumblings came from Mr. Darnek's raspy throat, as a whisper, then a roar. The breeze caught up his vile words, and I could not tell if they were from him, or the imagination of my own tortured mind:

"Bikini Summer Girl, bloody rags make me hurl...."

I pulled the blinds and hurried to my bed, where I hid beneath the sheets, trembling. I fell into a troubled sleep.

The next morning, I awakened sweaty and hot. I reached for my eyeglasses on the bedside table, forgetting that Sam still had them. Angrily, I threw off the sheets, and fumbled into clean shorts and a T-shirt. From the kitchen came the meaty smell of Swanson's TV dinners cooking in the oven. I hadn't eaten anything since lunch the day before. I snuck downstairs, hoping to avoid Gordon and the boys. Nobody was to be seen except my mom, who was mixing a green salad on the counter. I wondered if she would notice that I wasn't wearing my glasses.

"Where is everybody?" I asked cautiously.

"The boys are sleeping. Gordon went to work."

"Oh."

She gazed down at the wooden bowl, mindlessly tossing with wooden spoons the iceberg lettuce, carrots, and tomatoes.

"Did we keep you up last night?" she asked, looking down, still methodically stirring. She had not noticed that I wasn't wearing my glasses.

"It was pretty noisy."

"Yeah, I made Gordon mad."

"Oh?"

"I poured out all the wine and most of the beer."

"Why?"

"He drinks too much. I'm tired of it."

She walked to the sink and washed her hands. Barely audible above the running water, she said, "Get yourself a dinner out of the oven and some salad." With a towel she rubbed her fingers dry, and turned to face me. It was the first time that our eyes had met. She had an expression of worry and exasperation. I thought that she had noticed my missing eyeglasses, which were expensive to replace. She wouldn't believe me if I told her that Sam had stolen them. I hastily thought of the excuse that I had left them in the basement, but before I could speak, she interrupted.

"Oh, by the way, your dad is picking you up this afternoon."

"Really?"

"He's taking you to his place at the Lake. When Gordon gets off work in a couple of days, we're going up to the Lake, too," she said. "We haven't had a vacation in a long time."

They had never gone to the Lake during one of my visits with my father. "We'll be at a hotel in Lakemore—with the boys," she added. "Not far from your dad's place. Try not to bother them, okay?"

I nodded and put oven mitts on my hands, reaching into the oven for a silver tray of meatloaf and mashed potatoes. It was futile to tell my mom anything about my glasses. I would have to wait until the boys left their subterranean lair, and hope that I could sneak downstairs and find them later.

The morning passed quickly and the boys stayed in the basement while I packed my suitcase for the trip to Lakemore. When it was time for my father to arrive, I waited with my bag behind the front porch trellis, concealed by a tangled web of dying roses. The flowers were withering more from neglect than the heat. Since Gordon had come to live with us, my mother had abandoned gardening. Just like she had abandoned the books she had once loved.

As I waited, my mother came out on the front porch.

"Here," she said, coldly, handing me a neat, square bundle of envelopes tied with twine. "I've been saving these for you." The envelopes carried the return address of my father. "I just forgot," she said dismissively. "Do what you want with them."

"Why did you keep them from me?" I blurted out, before realizing that my surprised outburst might invite an argument. But my mother did not react as I expected. Instead, her shoulders relaxed, and she looked down at her feet, as if she were experiencing a sudden illumination of conscience.

"I don't know, Marabel. I've done some crazy things. Maybe it's time to start doing the right thing."

She turned and went back inside, while I stared at the clean white packet of letters my father had been sending me for two years. I opened the zippered side pocket of my suitcase and softly slid them in.

Suddenly, Kent and Sam raced up the side path from their

basement hideout. They commenced playing a rowdy game of Cowboys and Indians, shooting imaginary arrows and bullets at one another. Sam arrogantly wore my glasses, upside down. When my father roared into the driveway in his old Mercury, Kent yelled, "It's the sheriff!"

"Better throw her in jail!" Sam said, pointing at me behind the trellis. "She's a criminal with blood on her pants! "The joke caused the boys to erupt in laughter. Ken drew a slingshot from his pocket and picked up a rock. Aiming at my father's car, he said, "You'll never catch us alive!"

The rock bounced harmlessly off the hood as the boys sprinted down the street, whooping, *"Bikini Summer Pin-Up Girl, bloody rags make me hurl!"*

My father gazed after them, speechless.

"Hi, Dad," I said, stepping out from behind the trellis.

When he saw me, he bounded up to the porch. "Are you bleeding?" he asked with concern. "Did they hurt you?"

"No," I said. "They're just boys, being stupid."

He bowed down to kiss my forehead. His tanned, dark-haired forearm, showing beneath the rolled-up sleeves of his white shirt, rested gently against my forehead, and the cool shadow of his form was respite from the heat. The air around him was fragrant with Old Spice cologne. After he kissed me, he asked, "Where are your glasses?"

"I don't know."

"Was one of those boys wearing your glasses?"

"I don't know."

In the silence that ensued, I knew that he was thinking about what to do, and I hoped that he was not thinking of starting an inquisition. After a few moments he said, "We'll talk about this later. Let's get on the road."

We drove in silence, the 150 miles from Duane to Lakemore, distracted by our separate thoughts. I soaked in the pastoral scene of the familiar farmlands dotted with haystacks and grazing sheep and the waving stands of tall trees reaching to the azure sky. I wondered about the letters. Occasionally, I glanced at my father's profile, thinking about what he might have written, curious to ask questions, but content to simply sit and think about it. Peace had returned to my heart.

When we arrived at his small house in Lakemore, my father unlocked the door and carried my suitcase inside. He left me to unpack in the pleasant solitude while he went to the grocery store. My farsightedness had served me well, because I could see at distances without my glasses; close up reading, or nearby faces, were hazy. I would have taken up a book and begun reading, but without my glasses, that happy prospect was impossible.

Instead, I emptied my suitcase and put everything in drawers. I wandered through the rooms, plumping the well-worn couch pillows, gazing in awe at the sumptuous shelves of books, peeking through the sheer curtains at the well-loved and tended rosebushes outside of the front windows. The masculinity of the square edged furniture, leathery and well-used, and the antique tools displayed on a long workbench on the porch, spoke of my father's strength. These married well with the hints of glorious domestic touches, throughout. There were fresh wildflowers in a vase on the dining table, and the clean hardwood floors glowed as if scrubbed by strong hands, and everywhere there was the green scent of the outdoors invited in by open windows, mingling with the lingering fragrance of my father's Old Spice cologne.

The only thing that could tamp down my joy was the thought of mom, Gordon, and the boys arriving in a couple of days.

When my father returned, we prepared supper together, eating at the dining table where I could easily turn my head to see the rose bushes through the front windows. My father noticed.

"Do you like my garden?" he asked.

I nodded, sighing. "Yes. Our rose bushes are dying."

"I saw."

We ate in silence for a while, then he said, "I hear that Maggie and Gordon are bringing those boys up here Tuesday. Staying at a hotel. A vacation of sorts."

"How did you know?"

"She called me before I left to pick you up."

Although I said nothing, my sullen face must have indicated my unhappiness, because my father said, "They'll be on the other side of town. You'll be here with me. We'll go to the Lake together and swim when they aren't around." He paused, and added, "Don't worry about your glasses. I'm going to get some new ones for you."

"Thank you, dad."

I thought about his letters.

"If I want to read something, you know, a book or something, before then, what should I do?" I asked.

He got up and walked over to the rolltop desk by the side windows. Opening a small drawer, he pulled out several magnifying glasses.

"Perhaps these will do?" he said.

That night, after my father had gone to bed, I got out the letters. I held each magnifying glass over the crisp papers until I found one that worked. I bent over the pages, reading. The first letter had been written only days after he had left us:

"*I'm sorry I left without saying goodbye. Please forgive me...*"

This was the letter that he must have meant. I quickly took out the letter I had received in August and compared it with this, the first note in the packet. Yes, he had rewritten it and sent it to me in August. It was the only letter I had taken from the mailbox. My mother had hidden all the others.

Then, there was a short note, scribbled hastily, around the time that Gordon and mom married in our backyard.

"*I will always wear my wedding ring, to show that I believe in marriage. I hope that you will always believe in marriage, too....*"

At Christmas, he wrote:

"*I believe in miracles. Do you?*"

There were two-years of notes from every month of the year, and each had been written carefully in his firm, cursive handwriting; and each ended with the same closing:

"*I pray that God will bring us all together again someday....*"

I fell asleep in tears, with the pages in my hands, a dozen letters spilling over my chest and onto the bed.

The next day, I decided to keep the letters a secret from my father.

To reveal that my mother had kept them would only wound him. His written words were enough for me.

The day passed in a hazy summer's warmth, with a cool breeze stirred up by the rotating fans inside. I enjoyed the luxury of eating three homecooked meals with my father. His comforting presence made me forget about the terror of the boys. His mysterious letters read the night before made me forget about the two years of separation and silence.

At supper, my father said that he would be working as chaplain during the night shift at the local hospital.

"Don't be afraid," he said. "This is a sleepy little town. Keep the doors locked and the porch light on. I'll be home by the time you wake up in the morning."

"What about the boys? They're coming tomorrow, right?"

"Yes. But they will be on the other side of town. I'll be here with you, and when I'm not, you can keep the doors locked."

Late in the evening, I was sprawled on the couch, thumbing through an encyclopedia, looking at the fuzzy pictures, when my father walked into the room. He wore slacks and a dress shirt tucked into his pants, and the shiny black leather shoes he used to wear when he preached. He leaned over and kissed my forehead.

"Your appointment with the eye doctor is tomorrow. Be sure to leave the front lights on. I'll see you in the morning."

After he left, I pulled the blinds down, flicked on the outdoor light, and climbed the stairs to my bedroom. The black sky clouded the stars and moon, darkening the room. I flipped the switch of the bedside lamp, and in the bright, circular glow, I gathered all of my father's letters, which I had left lying on the bedspread. Without changing into pajamas, I crawled beneath the covers and read them again with the magnifying glass. This time, when I finished, I gathered them carefully and placed them in the drawer of the bedside table.

I lay in the friendly light of the lamp, thinking about the nightly routine. How different it was with my father. If my father had been with me, he might have sat in the wingback chair beside my bed, sharing a prayer from the Roman Breviary, which he had begun to read since moving to Lakemore. He said he had been given the book by a friend of his at the hospital.

"I am not really Catholic," he would say, opening to nightly Vespers in the *Liturgy of the Hours*, "But my heart finds comfort in these readings."

Sleepless and worried, I looked up at the ceiling for a long time. The longer I stayed awake, the more I frightened myself with terrible images of Kent and Sam, breaking my glasses and ripping off my swimsuit. I decided to pray the only prayer I had ever memorized:

"Now I lay me down to sleep, I pray the Lord my soul to keep. And if I die before I wake, I pray the Lord my soul to take."

I asked the Lord to keep my father, too.

Then I asked for something so outrageous that it could only be considered a childish fantasy at best, a delusion, at worst.

"God," I said, "If it's possible…if you don't mind…somehow, could you put us all together again? Would you answer my father's prayer?"

I turned off the lamp and laid back upon my pillow, pulling up the cool sheets. From behind the sheer curtains, a soundless pulse of lightning erupted in the darkness. It flashed rhythmically, like the notes of an evening lullaby. As the gentle storm blew through, I fell asleep.

I was awakened by a frantic banging on the front door downstairs. I opened my eyes, startled. Sunlight spilled through my windows, indicating mid-morning. Perhaps it was my father, who had lost his keys? I wrapped myself in a light blanket and ran down the steps to the living room. I peeked through the window beside the door, hiding behind the curtain's delicate, lacy veil.

A thin, nasally voice sounded from the other side.

"Marabel? Marabel Robinson?"

A man I didn't know stood by the door. I wondered, how did he know my name? I squinted. There was enough distance between us to see that he was a short, rather dowdy-looking man, wearing glasses and a black suit with white collar.

"My name is Father Jack," he said, knocking again. "I'm a friend of your dad, Ben Robinson. We work together at the hospital. I'm the Catholic chaplain."

He reminded me of a timid cat, circling a food bowl, unsure of whether to approach. He stepped back, as if he were turning to leave. I thought he was giving up, but then, with resolve, he stepped forward once more and knocked louder, announcing in a firm tone, "Your father sent me. He has an urgent message about your mom."

His words overcame my caution. I revealed my face through the window.

"Marabel?" he asked.

I nodded.

"Ben—I mean your father—sent me to tell you...there's been an accident..."

I unlocked the door and opened it.

He motioned to the porch swing.

"Maybe, well, maybe you better sit down."

Father Jack took the wicker chair across from the porch swing, where I sat nervously. "Your mom is okay...but the other...well, she and Gordon were in a car accident last night. They were on the way to Lakemore." When I began to cry, he went silent, offering his clean, white handkerchief.

"But I thought that they were coming today," I said, wiping my face. "Not driving last night. Why did they have to do that? It was stupid!" I knew that Gordon's nightly routine included drinking a few beers.

"I suppose that would have been preferable, driving in the day. Perhaps the accident wouldn't have happened," said Jack, thoughtfully.

As morning revolved into afternoon, Jack calmly told me the story, with the objectivity of a journalist. The heat thickened around me, making me sweat, but I hardly noticed.

He told me that my mother and Gordon had crashed on a road ten miles outside of Lakemore. That there had been a two-lane bridge across a dry creek bed. It had been a black night, and they had been driving through an especially dark part of the countryside.

I learned that the bridge had narrowed and that Gordon, who was driving, had not seen the narrowing. The bridge tapered inward, but Gordon's hands had stayed heavy on the wheel, forcing the vehicle straight ahead.

The right-side tires tracked up the inclining rails like a roller coaster roaring up a hill, picking up speed. Gordon's foot slammed on the accelerator, and they sped along, suspended in air, but hooked to the rails of the bridge, looking as if they were flying. There was one car coming the other way, and the driver saw it all.

The energy of their flight did not have the impetus to take them safely to the other side. Halfway across the bridge, with a sudden wrenching and groaning of metal, the tires slipped and the sedan sheared off the rails. They plunged off the right side of the bridge, thirty feet through the darkness, landing upside down, rolling several times through the cattails and long grasses of the dry stream below.

Gordon was killed instantly.

The boys were spared because they had not been in the car. Gordon and mom had decided not to bring them. They had dropped them off at the home of Gordon's ex-wife before the journey started.

My mother, bruised and unconscious, had been trapped in the crushed car. If not for the man who had happened to be driving by and seen it all, who rushed to the vehicle and pulled her out, she might still be bleeding at the bottom of the dry creek in a mangled car hidden in a thicket of weeds and grasses.

The man climbed the grassy hill to the neighbor's house to call for help. An ambulance transported my mother with a neck brace on a hard stretcher to the Lakemore Hospital. She had been brought in while my father was making his rounds as a chaplain. When he discovered she was there, he quickly went to her bedside, staying with her through the night.

"She'll have at least one, maybe two, surgeries," said Jack. "But the prognosis is good. She'll need lots of nursing care for a while."

He looked down at the rose bushes, and said softly, "Your father is a good man. I don't know many men who would do the same for their ex-wife."

As I slowly pushed the porch swing back and forth with my feet, I cast my gaze downward, to my hands clasped tightly on my lap. I remembered seeing the wedding ring still on my father's hand when he left the night before.

My mother did not leave the hospital for four weeks. Hers would be a lengthy recovery, and she had no place to go, for the house in Duane had entered bankruptcy courts. There was no one there to take care of her, anyway. My father offered her the spare room downstairs. She came to live with us, as a visitor would, recovering in the guest room off the kitchen.

Her legs had been badly injured, wrists broken, and her entire body bruised and lacerated. There were other, deeper injuries, we would not know of until many months later. She came to us in a wheelchair and stayed in bed for several days. I hardly recognized her puffy, blue-yellow face and swollen eyes. It was strange, having both my father and mother in the same house, again. Though they stayed apart, they were never far from one another. In the kitchen I could see my father preparing dinner on the stove at the same time that I glimpsed through the open door of her bedroom, the face of my mother, resting in her bed.

Gone were the angry creases and frustrated thinness of her lips. Instead, her face was darkened by a perpetual shadow of suffering. I could see distinctly her closed eyes, tightening and releasing with every wave of pain. Now that I was wearing the new eyeglasses that my father had bought for me, I could see clearly. I wondered if my prayer had been the cause of the accident.

My father's friend, the Catholic chaplain, Jack, would come to visit us occasionally. He and my father would sit at the kitchen table, talking soberly and drinking mugs of steaming coffee late into the night. When my mother began to feel better, she would call for Father Jack to sit at her bedside and say a prayer for her before he left.

One night, as I was lounging on the couch reading a book, my dad and Jack came through the living on their way to the front door. They had been discussing theology and philosophy for hours at the kitchen table, going through a pot of coffee and a box of donuts. When they reached the porch, I jumped up and followed them.

"Father Jack," I said timidly. "Could you…I mean, could I ask you something?"

"Of course," he said.

"Just you," I said, glancing at my father.

My father looked surprised, but then he said, "Goodnight, Jack. Marabel, be sure to lock the front door when you come inside."

Jack seated himself comfortably in the wicker chair. I went to the porch swing and sat facing Jack, the way I had the morning he came to tell me about the accident. The warm light of lanterns on each side of the door formed a pleasant circle around the two of us.

"I feel really bad," I said. "I prayed something that night. You know, the night when the car went off the bridge?"

I faltered.

"What did you pray?" he asked softly.

"I prayed…I asked God if he would—If he would—"

The embarrassment and shame I felt made it difficult to speak, the words coming haltingly at first. Finally, my thoughts spilled out in a torrent of emotions.

"I didn't mean it to be this way! I mean for Gordon, for him to, you know…." I inhaled sharply and continued. "Was it my fault? All I did was ask God to bring us back together, me and my mom and Dad, but I didn't mean for my mom to get hurt! I never liked Gordon. I—I kind of hated him. But I didn't wish—I didn't wish for anybody to *die*."

I began to cry.

Father Jack handed me his white handkerchief. He remained silent for a while. The only sounds were my sniffling and the swishing of the brown leaves of the autumn trees.

He said, "Perhaps, you feel guilty because you wished you didn't have Gordon in your life?"

"Yes," I whispered, with tears.

He nodded and said, "Prayers are not wishes."

I tilted my head and scrunched my eyebrows. "What do you mean?"

"Well," he said, leaning back and looking up at the sky beyond the porch. "Sometimes, people wish on stars, or throw pennies into wells. They want something, but it's often selfish. Wishes are those fleeting emotions that we often later recant."

"If I could take it back, I would!" I cried. I turned my face towards the yard. Above the trees, thin clouds whisked by, bringing a sudden breeze that ruffled the rose bushes beside the porch and cooled my face.

Father Jack continued, "Wishes and prayers are different. A prayer is the cry of the heart. It's the heart that desires what God desires, wants what He wants, even if we cannot quite fathom what we are asking for."

"I wanted my parents to be together—all of us, together."

"You wanted something good. Your family together, your parents together. God wants that too."

"Really?

"Yes. He is the author of marriage."

"But why…"

For a few moments there was silence between us. I listened as a mourning dove couple cooed from their nest. Their mournful cries became the notes played above the rhythm of the creaking porch swing as I pushed back and forth. I feared that I had asked a question he could not answer. Father Jack at last spoke.

"There were other prayers…other hearts…involved," he said. "Who knows? Only God knows what was best for all."

He sighed deeply and looked down at his hands. "You see, Marabel, we cannot always understand why things turn out the way they do. But we can always believe that God has a loving purpose in it."

He leaned forward and grasped my hands. His eyes were bright with a luminous kind of courage. "Find God's loving purpose in this, Marabel, and you will be healed."

For several weeks, a nurse visited daily, until my mother was able to leave the bedroom, using a cane. She sat with us for brief moments at the dining table. My father would read to us aloud from the *Liturgy of the Hours*, for it had now become his regular routine. My mother would eat and listen, quietly, without interruption. The fear of her past outbursts kept me anxious, my muscles tight with the readiness to run from the room if she tried to spar with me or my father. But she said nothing. Sometimes, I saw a curious expression of surprise pass over her face as she gazed at my father. It was as if she were discovering him, for the first time.

In the evenings, she joined us in the living room, sitting quietly, wrapped in a blanket on the couch, observing us as we discussed philosophy or played a competitive game of checkers. Mostly, she read books from my father's library. Her old love for literature was slowly blooming, and she picked up whatever book my father had left open on the side table. She rarely spoke, until it was time to say, "Good-night."

I asked my father one evening after she had gone to bed, "What is wrong with mom?"

"She had surgery, remember?"

"No, I mean, why doesn't she talk much anymore? She reads books. She doesn't argue or complain."

"Tragedy has a way of changing a person," he said.

"Do you think she has really changed?"

"I've always thought it was possible. A wise man once said, *faith is to believe what you do not see. The reward of faith is to see what you believe.*"

"Who said that?"

My father smiled and tousled my hair. " Saint Augustine of Hippo."

It was mid-autumn, just before the winter cast its chill upon the land and snow hemmed us into our house. My mother insisted on walking to the Lake. She had not walked that far since her release from the hospital.

"Would you both go with me?" she asked in a timid voice.

"Yes, Maggie, we will go with you."

My father got her jacket and his, and I filled a thermos with hot coffee and a tin with cookies. Bundled in our coats, we started the journey down the road. My father stayed on her right and I on her left. Holding his arm with one weak hand and using a cane with the other, my mother limped painfully along, shuffling through the swirling red and orange leaves blown by a chilly breeze. My father steered us around the pavement's crevices and dips, keeping us on a plain, steady path. A trip that normally took ten minutes, lasted almost half an hour. By the time we reached the park bench overlooking Erie, my mother was exhausted.

Father held both her arms as she lowered herself slowly to the bench. We joined her, sitting side by side, with my mother in the middle. Without speaking, we drank the coffee and ate the cookies. We watched the white-capped waves roll in before the first winter storm. Above us, the bruised sky filled with clouds of icy rain, poised to become snow. Before us, the Lake pounded the rocky beach below the cliff. We sat, as observers, safely above it on the park bench. It was hard to believe that this was the same Lake that had once buoyed me gently on a floating carriage built by a King for his Mermaid-Princess. Behind us the enormous oak tree, where we had shared picnic lunches, now braced itself against the whipping wind.

There we sat, a circle of three, a family, in the solitude of our hearts. We were silent before the noise of foaming purl and rushing wind. The song of the coming storm filled the emptiness inside of me; the closeness of my mother and father now bridged the chasm that had once been deeper than the heart of Erie. A new feeling, a nascent stirring of love, rooted within me, strengthening me. I felt the hope of a child who yearns for the eternal circle of her parent's embrace.

Then, my mother spoke.

"It is good to be here," she said.

Gone was the harshness of her voice that I had become accustomed to. In the smallest of whispers, I heard my father answer. "Yes, it is."

Christmas came, and my mother stayed. We unwrapped gifts from under the tree. We ate the homecooked meal my father made, of roast and potatoes, rolls and green beans, pecan pie and eggnog, until we could hold no more.

My mother said she felt unwell. She ate little, but sat across from us at the table, smiling with a contentment that I had not seen in many years.

"I'm tired," she said.

My father had a worried expression. "Should I call the nurse?" he asked.

"No."

He helped her up from the chair and handed her the cane.

"Good night," she said. Before entering her darkened bedroom, she turned to look at us. The furrowed lines of pain on her face had softened, and a tender light glimmered in her dark eyes.

"I'm sorry," she breathed. "I am truly sorry, Ben. Can you…will you…forgive me?"

My father, who had been standing by the table, took a few halting steps towards her, until he could move no more. He fell to his knees before her, uttering deep, guttural cries that shook his body.

"All is forgiven," he wept, *"forgiven…"*

She put one frail hand upon his head. Then she said with a trembling voice, "Marabel, come…"

I jumped up from my seat and ran to her, embracing her with both arms. My father reached up and grasped my hand and hers; together, we formed a circle of flesh and blood and tears.

We never returned to live again in Duane. I never again saw Kent and Sam, whose mother moved them somewhere south, closer to the ocean. I did not leave my father's house in Lakemore, but stayed, attending the school there until I graduated four years later.

My mother lived with us for another year, and we took many walks with my father to the Lake. Though they slept in separate bedrooms, my parents spent the evenings together in the living room where they discussed the books they were reading, while I did homework at the dining table. I overheard their conversations, reminiscing over memories, with tears—sometimes they laughed, and always before the evening ended, they held hands and prayed together. If I had not yet gone to bed, I joined them.

The winter before my 14th year, my father asked me to come with him to a Mass at the parish where Father Jack served. It was the midnight Christmas Eve service, filled with candlelight and incense, of sacred prayers and liturgy. I went with curiosity and a sense of expectation. It was strange to see my father, once the pastor of his own congregation, kneeling on the other side of the altar, like all the rest of us.

We hoped my mother would come with us, but she was feeling unwell. Although she had grown stronger, she was not strong enough to overcome the deeper injuries in her body. Tired and weak, she stayed behind.

When my father and I returned to the house, her room was dark. I went upstairs and fell asleep quickly. I awakened Christmas morning to a curious stillness. A soft and cloudy snow was falling quietly outside my windows. I went downstairs into the kitchen, hoping to see my mother through the door of her bedroom. I looked forward to opening the curtains so that she could enjoy the fresh layer of snow covering trees and yard. But first, I would surprise her with a cup of coffee.

Humming "Joy to the World," I poured water into the coffee pot and took two mugs from the cabinet, gathered the sugar bowl and pitcher of cream. Her room was strangely silent.

"Mom?"

I peered around the corner of her bedroom door. I was surprised to see my father sitting on the edge of the bed, holding my mother's hand. In the golden light of the bedside lamp, I could see that her eyes were closed, and her pale face, which once held grooves of deep suffering, now glowed serenely.

Gently, my father picked up her other hand and placed both tenderly over her heart. Then he bent his head and sobbed.

No words were needed. I knew my mother was gone. I rushed to my father's side, falling to my knees by the bed, weeping. His strong, square hand grasped mine.

"She passed away, Marabel, in the night...*she passed away...*"

Outside her bedroom windows, I could hear the faintest sound of the wind catching the snow in its arms.

Many decades have gone by since my mother's death on Christmas Eve.

I am an old woman, now.

Sometimes, I return to Erie in the summer. I stand upon the cliff overlooking the green tide. I cast about in my mind for the images of those days,when we swam together in the cold water, and I can almost taste, once again, the spray and splash in my laughing mouth and hear my father's bass voice joining mine. I can see my mother waving to us, calling us to come to the picnic beneath the old oak tree.

I can no longer traverse the steep slope to the sandless shore. Instead, I stand for as long as I am able and then I sit on the park bench where my father and mother first fell in love, where they dreamed their dreams of the future, overlooking the Lake. It was the hand of Providence who returned them, bringing us all together, a circle of three.

I hear the voices of the boulders singing in the joy of the dawn, and the cries of the hungry gulls winging through the blue sky, and the thunder of the clouds growing larger and heavier with rain. I look down at the treacherous rocky battlefields below and remember how the strength of my father kept us from stumbling and falling on our way to the water.

If ever there were a Lake that could turn you into a mermaid, it would be Erie. If ever there were a father who could turn you into a Princess, it would be mine. He was King of the Lake, and my mother was the true love of his heart.

THE BEARDED MAN

When a stranger passes by the house, with its sagging porch and overgrown wild-grasses, they shake their heads and ask me, "Who lives there?"

And I say, "Nobody. I live next door to nobody."

And then they look at the mulberries and sycamores with their dying branches and the boards across the broken windows, and they say, "Why doesn't somebody tear it down?"

And I say, "You can't tear down a monument."

And then they laugh and go on laughing all the way down the street, saying, "Nobody in their right mind would think an old house like this is a monument." But then a few stay around and ask me, "What makes this a monument?"

I say, "Because a great man lived here. A man and his son. And I knew them."

Then I tell them about Joe and his boy.

The boy was three when he came to live with Joe and Susan and the two other children who were born from Susan, but had different daddies. Joe brought the boy home to be a part of that mixed-up family. Joe wanted to be daddy to all of them.

It was back in the days when the house was painted white with blue shutters. There was glass in those windows. And you wouldn't know it now, but there were climbing roses. They grew all over those porch rails, reaching and wanting to grow right up to the front door.

When Joe came home with the boy, he brought the child riding on top of his big, wide shoulders, and he carried him right up those porch steps calling out his new name—

Samuel.

It was beautiful the way he said it.

At the sound, the boy's face stretched out, like a flower after a droughted summer, like a tiny thing barely hanging on, as if it had never seen a hard-soaked rain and didn't know much what to do with it except open.

At night, Joe sat in the middle of the floor with the three children hanging on him, laughing and rolling off and on his big-bellied lap while he read to them from a book. Samuel liked the pictures of the man who looked like Joe, but with a beard. The bearded man had saved his family and all the married animals from drowning.

When Joe took Samuel to the biggest church in town, the church where he worked as a maintenance man—when he brought his newly-named boy for the first time, this child looking so different from Joe—the people said, "Oh, what a *nice* boy," as if you couldn't say anything else without being nosy and maybe gossipy, and there was some sort of commandment against it, and so you didn't ask. You just *looked.*

The pastor said nothing. He didn't even look. But when he grabbed Joe's hand after the service to shake it, the pastor's fat fingers, with all the jeweled rings, skimmed right over the boy's head, touching the hair that stood up in curly bunches. When Joe and his boy walked away, I saw the pastor take out a handkerchief from his pocket and scrub all of his fingers like a woman would scrub a stain off her Sunday dress.

Samuel had skin smooth and dark, like the best coffee served without cream. Joe had skin that was rosy and glowed like a sunset against the sandstone sky in the desert.

"We are a forever family," Joe said. "Call me *Daddy.*"

Susan didn't want to be called *Mommy.* She said, "Call me *Susan.*"

She didn't much like making lunch for those children. If she ever did, it wasn't much. Mostly it was sandwiches. She slapped bologna between slices of bread. No mustard. No mayonnaise. She shoved the plates at the children and went back to her bedroom. She'd say, "I'm going to bed. I have a headache."

Every morning she took a bottle of beer out of the fridge and drank it. One morning when she ran out, she lied to the children and said, "I'm going to the store. I'll get you some popsicles."

That was a humid day, as I recall. The three children kept close to the fan in the living room and watched TV. The sun jumped up to the top of the sky, and I believe it burned a hole right through the roof. The day got hotter. The room got kind of wobbly—you know, the kind of wavy heat you see coming out of an oven? It was that kind of day. They sweated. Their stomachs hurt.

So, they decided to go into the kitchen where there weren't so many windows, and a bigger fan, and they made some peanut butter sandwiches. No jelly. They were out of jelly. When they got pretty full, they went back into the living room and fell asleep on the couch. About the time the sun got down to the edge of the street, they woke up, and through the window they could see it melting everywhere, making them think of a red popsicle, and then they saw Joe walking through the door, coming home from work.

He opened the pantry and found a can of chicken noodle soup and a box of crackers. He poured the can into a pan and heated it on the stove. He shook the last drops of milk from a plastic jug into three small cups, and set the box of saltines on the table and called the children, who climbed onto the chairs. That soup tasted so good—even if it was hot on a hot day. They made happy slurping sounds with the noodles and crammed crackers into their mouths. All the time, Joe didn't eat. He stood at the window, staring at the empty street. After a while, he said, "I'll be back."

"Popsicles, Daddy?" asked Samuel.

"Yes," said Joe.

They watched him leave the house in his truck. Samuel cried.

The night fell all over the place, the way somebody shakes out a box of checkers on the floor. It had a sound, sort of a roaring noise, like the ocean, the one they call the Gulf of Mexico, way down to the south, you know? The children had been there once. Seen the water and the waves. That noise and those dark checker shadows came up on the house and took it over the way the water comes up on the beach and takes over the sand. There was heat lightning, which is worse than the real thing, and a trembling moon that glowed eerie and strange behind the clouds. Those trees you see there? They were giants, with shields and swords, fighting back and forth, all dark and dancing.

The children turned up the TV. That way, they couldn't hear the banging noises of those branches, fighting with each other and slapping the house. When they got sleepy, they brushed their teeth, because that's what Joe taught them to do, and they put on their pajamas, but they didn't want those blankets on them because it was still too hot in the house. That wasn't the worst part, though. The worst part was that they went to bed without a story.

Samuel cried.

All that night Susan stayed away. They were used to Susan being away. But Joe didn't come back, either, and Joe never did that. When they woke up, Joe and Susan still weren't there. They were scared and hungry. They went into the kitchen and made peanut butter sandwiches with the last pieces of dry bread and scraping the sides of the peanut butter jar till it was empty, and they sat down at the table wondering if that was their last meal.

All of a sudden, they heard someone banging on the front door. They jumped up from that table so fast you would have thought there'd been a tornado comin' through. They jumped up and hid behind that gigantic old, couch in the living room. They could see a large woman through the windows. She was a piece of work. You could tell she had strong bones, because she was pounding flat-handed against that door and making the kind of noise that could wake the dead. Her face was stump-nosed, splotch-skinned, with a jaw that was more flabby skin than bone. She wore a flowered dress and a bright red belt that tied under her bosom and made her look fatter than she was. Nobody else knew who she was—but Samuel knew, and he was scared.

Right then, Joe's old truck pulled up into the driveway. He parked next to the woman's gray Buick and got out. The children ran to the window and watched. Joe and that woman, they came together in the middle of the yard, the way two prize fighters meet in the ring, kind of circling each other, waiting to see who would punch first with words. The children couldn't hear any of the words, but they saw the woman's flowery dress jiggling up and down because she was waving her arms and yelling so much, and her head was bobbing around like a fish on a hook.

Joe's face was a river stone. It was hard, with all the red sunset colors washed away. He was taller, so he stared down at the woman with his chin stuck out. The woman turned and pointed her finger at the house. Joe pointed to her car and waved to the east, as if telling her to go that way, far away, far, far away, *now.* She shook a folder of papers at him. She pushed the papers at Joe, who took them. Then she stomped along the sidewalk to the driveway. She had those kind of clunky shoes that clumped hard, making that *thwacking* noise that makes your ears hurt—you know, the way the woman next door takes a broom to beat the blankets on the clothesline? That was the sound she made.

After she left, Joe came into the house. He was carrying the folder and a paper bag. He stopped in the door looking like the most friendly grizzly bear you ever saw, but sad, really sad. He was so big and tall and sad that you couldn't see the sun, because he was one, big bear shadow.

"Daddy!"

Samuel ran over and grabbed Joe's legs and held on.

"Popsicles," Joe said, holding out the paper bag.

The children shouted and screamed and opened the plastic wrappers and put those icy-cold popsicles on their tongues and let it drip down their chins, and they laughed because it tasted so good.

The children didn't know that Joe had been up all night, looking for Susan. They didn't know that Joe had found her in the same place he'd found her before, in that gray, ugly building on top of the hill. You know which one I mean? Not the jailhouse. The place they take people who aren't in their right minds. The place where they put you in that faded dress that smells like Clorox, that ties in the back. The place where you look at somebody through a glass window and can't touch them. That's where Joe found Susan.

This time, they told Joe he couldn't bring Susan home.

Maybe, not ever.

They shoved some papers at him and told him to sign them.

Then they called in the woman in the flowered dress and red belt. That stump-nosed, saggy-jawed woman.

She said, "In the morning I'll come to the house and get the boy."

Joe didn't know what to do, so he left that ugly building on the hill. He left Susan there because he couldn't take her home anyway, and he drove his truck all around the town, driving from one end to the other and back, just so he could think.

The only thing he could think was to go see the pastor. When the sun came up, Joe pulled into the church parking lot and went inside. He sat in the pastor's office and told him everything. Joe felt about as desperate as a man could be. There wasn't much Joe could do except beg for help. And he begged. But that pastor wasn't feeling much helpful that day. You know what he said to Joe about Susan?

"*She got… what she… deserved.*"

Joe couldn't do anything about Susan.

He said, "What about the children?"

And the pastor said, "Give those two brats to Susan's family. But give the other boy back to the state."

Joe said, "I'm their Daddy, now."

The pastor said, "Well, not the boy. He's a foster brat. Give him up. If you want to keep your job, give him up."

Joe left the church that day in his truck feeling about as low as any man ever could, maybe even lower than that man in the Bible, you know, Job, who lost his kids and his wife? He was feeling that low.

Now, Joe wasn't going to let that woman take Samuel from him in front of the other two children. There's just some pain you can't give to others if you have the chance to spare them. That's why he sent her away when she showed up at the house. That's why he told her to go east. He was going to meet her somewhere else. But he was still going to give up Samuel.

Now, before you go judging Joe too hard, ask yourself, what could Joe do? Nobody was going to help him. Nobody. Not the pastor. Not those doctors in the gray building on top of the hill. And that woman in the flower-dress? She was coming over soon to take Samuel away.

Well, let's see, where was I? Oh, right, we were talking about Joe coming home from the church and scaring off the fat woman, and bringing popsicles to those poor children who hadn't had a decent meal in days. Joe waited for them to finish up their popsicles and then he told Samuel, "Let's go for a ride. Just you and me."

Usually, that was his way of saying, *Let's go to Wal-Mart*. Automatically, everybody thought about toys and candy. The other two children started running around the room hunting for matching shoes and pennies for the bubblegum machine, because they didn't hear Joe say, "Just you and me."

"Where?" asked Samuel. His bright eyes opened wide, like the doors of the boat that carried the man and his family and all of the married animals.

Joe had soft, watery eyes, that closed, like the earth swallowing all those other poor creatures that got left behind in the flood.

"Somewhere. Just you and me."

The other two children stopped looking for shoes and pennies.

He kissed their cheeks and patted their heads. Then, he took Samuel outside to his truck.

Joe and his boy drove that truck over all those bridges between here and Slidell, those tiny bridges going over sloughs and creeks and swampland, and through the town to their south with the tall buildings, and past those canals that the Dutch built between the houses. Those canals, you know, catch the rain so it doesn't flood. It's so flat here, it floods regular. And there are alligators in those canals. Samuel heard they came out at night and ate up small dogs.

One day, he asked, Joe, "Will alligators get me?" and Joe said, "Not unless they can get me first."

Well, Samuel didn't have to worry about any alligators when he was riding next to his Daddy in the truck.

The sun was hotter than Hades when Joe pulled into the Wal-Mart parking lot. He took off their seatbelts and picked up Samuel and put him down on the ground. Samuel had put some pennies in his pocket and was fishing around to get them together. He was going to get a football so he could pretend he was quarterback with his Daddy. Samuel was walking along with Joe, holding his hand and looking into his pocket. He didn't see the woman in the flowery dress with the red belt. His Daddy led him right up to that gray Buick where she was standing, smoking a cigarette. She threw it down and stomped on it with those big, clumpy shoes.

She squatted on her knees and put out her arms to the boy.

"Hello, Samuel," she said, in a voice that had a thick, scratchy sound like somebody's been smoking too much.

Samuel was too scared to do anything except stand there and open his mouth and make these little noises like a trapped baby animal does, if you've ever heard one, and I sure hope you never do.

The woman with the fish-hook head gives him a piece of candy. She says, "They don't want you no more, but somebody else gonna want you, baby."

And Joe just stands there, with his eyes shut.

Samuel opens his mouth to start crying and she drops a big caramel candy on his tongue so he has to chew, and she squeezes him hard with her big, fat arms and says, "Come with me, baby, somebody else gonna want you, *somebody that looks just like you.*"

Well, Joe isn't just standing there anymore. He's thinking. And he's feeling this grizzly bear kind of rage, if you know what I mean. Nobody'd accuse him of being friendly right about now. He's experiencing that kinda rage men feel when somebody burns down their house or steals their wife. It's a powerful kind of electricity in the body, but slow and burning. It starts in his heart and goes up to his arms and down his legs, and now he's strong enough to pull up a tree or wrestle an alligator.

That man, Joe, grabs the boy and sweeps him up into his arms with the power of a hurricane, spinning and crazy, and it makes the boy's legs jerk straight out and those tiny tennis shoes with big rubber soles, they kick that woman right in her stub-nose. Smacks her in that saggy, old face and knocks her down. Flat on her back.

Joe's got his boy. He gets him in the truck, puts on the seatbelts, and revs that engine up and makes the tires burn the road, he's going so fast.

You know what that woman is yelling? She couldn't get up off that parking lot to save her life, but she's yelling and screaming and twisting around and saying,

"The state's gonna take him back! He belongs to *us*! He ain't yours no more! *You ain't fit to be his daddy!*"

Samuel looks out the back window of the truck. He thinks for sure he is seeing an alligator. She's an inky, flower-dressed alligator squirming on the ground. And the faster Joe goes, driving away, far, far away, the smaller she gets, until the gray cement rises up like a giant wave and swallows her.

Samuel is the boy sailing away with the bearded man on the big boat.

This house, here?

Yup. It's a monument. You can see that now, can't you?

You're asking me how long it's been empty?

Since the night they all left.

That's right. Joe and his children, all three. He wasn't going to leave any of them behind. He came back here to this very house and packed them and a few things into his truck, and took them all away together. Sailed away to the edge of the world.

Changed their names.

I can't tell nobody their new names, but I can tell you this…

I have a friend who lives in Alaska. She works at a diner there in one of those little lumber and fishing towns. She said she looked up one day when the door chimes were jingling. They always do when somebody walks through the door. But this time, there was something different about them.

She said they were ringing like angel choirs.

Through that door walked a man as big and tall as the friendliest Grizzly bear you ever did see, and happy, too, and the sun walked right in with him, making the whole place bright. The man had skin the color of sunset in the winter, all rosy on the snow, and his brown, curly beard was looking freshly grown like he hadn't shaved in a few weeks.

And the angels' choirs were singing with the three children. Two of them were holding his hands and walking alongside him and they all laughed together.

And high up, almost touching the ceiling, was a boy, riding on top of the man's big, wide shoulders.

A boy with skin dark and smooth, like the best coffee without cream.

Her Best Kiss

Lilly's best kiss was not the one she got when she was five. Although, that was an interesting kiss.

She had endured it from her cousin, the only boy on her mother's side. It happened during a game of Hide and Go Seek. They were covered by a blanket, hiding inside of an enormous empty cardboard box. The other girl cousins counted to 100 and shouted, "Ready or not, here we come!"

They did not think to look inside the box. Instead, they searched the closets and behind tables. In the dark and stuffy box, Lilly's five-year-old cousin suddenly grabbed her and said, "Kissy, kissy!"

He put his wet lips on hers and made funny slurping noises. "Yuck!" she said.

"Ewww…," the girls had said when they found Lilly being kissed by their boy cousin in the cardboard box. The girl cousins ran upstairs and told his mother, Aunt Lucille. She had stiff blonde curls and tight religious morals. She stomped downstairs in her high heels and pulled her boy out of the box.

"Don't kiss your cousin!" she said, dragging him away by the ear.

Years later, Lilly began to notice how handsome her boy cousin was becoming, and she daydreamed about kissing him again. But on that day of their five-year-old kiss, her aunt had put the fear of hellfire in him with a good paddling. He never kissed her again.

Lilly's best kiss was not the one she got when she was sixteen. Although, it would be the first of many kisses.

The goalie of the soccer team had asked her to the high school dance. He was short and muscular, with brown hair and freckles, and he stuttered, especially around Lilly. After the prom, they stood awkwardly together on her front porch, holding hands.

"Mmm-m-may I kkk-k-k-kiss—you?" he stammered.

She nodded.

The kiss was soft and warm. Their lips barely touched before he pulled away and closed his eyes, sighing like a man who had just eaten the best steak with butter sauce and wanted to relish the moment before taking another bite.

Lilly felt like she had kissed the wrong person.

While the goalie contemplated kissing her again, she quickly opened the front door.

"Good-night," she said, disappearing inside.

Though she never kissed the goalie again, there were many other boys and many other dances and many other opportunities to kiss the wrong person.

Lilly's best kiss was not the one she got when she was twenty-four.

Although, that was supposed to be a forever kiss.

Her father had walked tall and proud beside her down the aisle, holding her arm, and taking shorter steps because his legs were much longer than hers. The satin wedding gown flowed behind her in a soft train, and the bouquet of peach-colored roses dropped fragrant petals along the way.

At the altar, her fiancé in his ivory suit with the peach tie took her hands in his. He lifted the gauzy veil. His blue-gray eyes seemed to say, "I will love you always," and her green-brown eyes answered, "I will always love you, too."

"I pronounce you husband and wife," said the pastor.

They tilted their heads at a specific angle, as they had practiced during rehearsal, to accommodate the various positions of the photographer who furiously snapped photos for future scrap books. Their lips touched lightly. Lilly believed there would be no more wrong kisses.

One day, Lilly found a note on the kitchen table. On the paper her husband had written that they were no longer husband and wife, that the marriage was over, that he had found someone else. It was her father who had come to Lilly's house after she found her husband's note, because she called him on the phone in tears, not knowing what to do. It was her father who had quietly packed her suitcases while she sat at the kitchen table crying. While her father put everything in the car, Lilly lingered behind, looking at her wedding photo on the wall, wishing that her husband had not decided that he had kissed the wrong person.

Lilly's best kiss came many years later.

It was the kiss of a grateful heart, although, at the time she did not realize that it was her best kiss.

It was a hot summer day at the brambly ranch where her sister lived with their father because he was becoming weak and needed care. Lilly had been invited to the outdoor birthday party for her fifteen-year-old niece. The pouty girl preferred to splash with her teen-aged friends in the pool, while the adults stood around sweating, telling jokes, grilling burgers and steaks, and spiking the lemonade with tequila.

Lilly found a shady spot beneath a blue, plastic tarp set up on four poles, making a shady pavilion. She sipped bottled water and observed everything through her sunglasses.

It wasn't long before she saw her father on the path beneath the mesquite trees, struggling to push his walker through the overgrown grass. He wore his customary newsboy cap on top of his balding head, his hunched-over body straining through the knee-high weeds towards the patch of sunlight and shorter grass beyond. In spite of the walker, he moved quickly, as if he were younger than the sickly eighty-seven-year-old man that he had become.

"Over here, dad," Lilly called. She stood up and helped navigate him towards the shade. Her father crumpled into a canvas lawn chair with a sigh.

It had been more than a year since they had been together.

They sat side by side all afternoon, drinking cold water, watching the teenagers and children play in the pool, waiting for the hamburgers and steaks to finish cooking.

They talked of the early years, when Lilly was a baby and they had lived in the farmhouse in Kansas. They laughed together, remembering how small she was, how she could walk under the kitchen table when she was three. Her father told her the story again of how she had grown an inch overnight and didn't know it and tried to walk under the table but hit her head and stepped back with a puzzled look of surprise.

As the day went on, Lilly brought them more cold water, and paper plates piled high with potato salad, pickled okra, and thick, juicy steaks. Between bites, her father reminisced about the early years of their lives. He told her how amazed he had been by her musical touch as she played Chopin, even though she had not won the piano contest. With napkins they wiped their eyes as they spoke of her mother, who passed away the year before. Her father recalled the day when Lilly was born. He told of the awe he felt when he held her in his arms and gave her newborn cheeks their very first kiss.

The shadows grew larger, and the day began to cool as the night whispered that it was near. The men were now scrubbing the barbecue grill, the children were crying because their mothers were calling them out of the pool, and the teenagers were telling jokes and eating leftovers around the picnic table.

Lilly reluctantly stood up.

"I have to go," she said.

She lived far away, and she knew that the drive would be long.

Her father looked at her with his blue-gray eyes now rimmed red.

"It's been good," he said, removing his cap, letting the cool evening air tousle the thin hair.

He reached his stiffened fingers towards her, taking her hands in his.

Lilly felt a sudden sadness within, like a cold gust of winter wind, making her tremble. Her thoughts turned to all of the years when she had ignored her dad and taken him for granted.

"I'm sorry, dad…" she whispered. Through her mind flittered all the memories of the times she had refused to pick up the phone when he had called, or hung up on him because she got mad—all the times she had rejected his good advice, or forgotten his birthday.

His lips curved upwards into a knowing smile that made the gray skin beneath his eyes become a dozen jagged lines of kindness.

"I love you, daughter," he said.

In a tender gesture, she leaned over and gently touched her lips to the top of his head, which was warm and soft, like baby's skin.

"I love you, too, dad."

She turned and made her way through the tangle of mesquite and tall grass, looking back once to see her father, still sitting in the canvas lawn chair. He saw her, and smiled. With one frail hand he slowly touched his fingers to his lips and silently made the gesture of a kiss blown on the breath of the evening breeze.

DREAMERS & SCHEMERS
The Power of Spunky Ole' Gals

It's not easy getting old. It takes courage, fortitude, and a whole lot of spunk. I've known a few older folks who've had the grit and determination to shake their fists at death, and say, "Come and get me!" Their stick-to-itiveness is a wonder to behold. From rodeo wheelchairs to wishin' stars, the gals in these stories never give up on their dreams. Even if it means getting swept out of the house by a hurricane in your easy chair.

Eudocia's Rebellion

"Each generation is converted by the saint who contradicts it most."

~G.K. Chesterton

Secret Life

"A dreamer is one who can only find his way by moonlight, and his punishment is that he sees the dawn before the rest of the world."

~Oscar Wilde

Too Much TV, You'll Go Blind

*May you live to be a hundred years
With one extra year to repent.*

~Irish toast

Eudocia's Rebellion

It is day 64 of the quarantine, and Eudocia is craving a grilled Rueben on rye. Never mind the wily virus supposedly stalking the maskless. Forget about the weatherman's predictions of rain or the fat, black clouds packing the western horizon. She's thinking about rolling her motorized wheelchair right out her front door and driving herself the ten miles to Luby's Cafeteria off I-35. At this point, even a tornado isn't going to hold her back. She can't stomach the idea of eating on the property one more day. To her mind, the kitchen food downstairs is too soft for real teeth, and she's mighty proud to still have a mouthful. She still has her tastebuds, too. The kitchen's food is flavorless as a cardboard box.

"I'm bustin' outta here," she says to her cat.

Before she can add, "Lickety-split," a voice erupts from the intercom system above her head. It's a one-way speaker connecting the manager's office to the 108 units of Sunny Grove, a 55-and-up apartment complex. Eudocia lives in a two-bedroom flat on the fourth floor overlooking the parking lot.

"Good morning, residents," says the bodiless voice in a fake-happy tone. Eudocia recognizes the voice as Lolly, one of the managers. *"I hope everyone is having a blessed and wonderful morning."*

Lolly's voice is louder than the Texas gully-washer getting ready to boom outside Eudocia's window—and more annoying. Wagging her long, crooked index finger at the ceiling, Eudocia huffs, "Well, it was *gonna* be a blessed and wonderful morning until *you* came along."

The voice from above continues unperturbed.

"Now, remember, we must stay in our apartments during this

quarantine. This wily virus is not finished making its rounds, and we don't want anybody to catch it."

"Harrumph! I never caught nothing in my life, except a dud of a husband," Eudocia quips. "And I got rid o' him."

"The dining room is open from 11:30 till 1, and today they're serving delicious fried catfish with Texas toast and sweet tea for only nine dollars."

"Fish too salty. Toast too soggy. Tea too sweet," Eudocia mumbles. "And I'm all out of Pepto-Bismol."

"If you want lunch to be delivered to your apartment, you've got to call them," says Lolly. *"Remember, only call them if you need it delivered, and don't call if you're coming down to the dining room. Call if you want it delivered. Again, if you want it to be delivered, please call."*

"Call you *what? Idiot?*" cackles Eudocia." Oh, wait, I'm the idiot because you have to remind me four times to call for delivery."

Eudocia is known—and usually avoided by most people—for her perennial sarcasm. Even her cat recognizes the irony in her voice and hides his head between his front paws.

Outside, the storm announces its arrival with a long timpani of thunder, followed by an off-beat staccato of hail that picks up speed as it pelts the windows of Eudocia's apartment.

"Just a friendly reminder to pick up after your pets. If you're at the dog park, be sure to clean up your pet's potty-mess. Nobody wants to step on that, and definitely it's not the job of my housekeeper to pick that up. Please make sure that you're taking your pets out and taking them to the pet potty station."

"Did you hear that, Johnny?" asks Eudocia, looking down at her cat. "Aren't you glad you're not a dog?"

"I know it's raining, but they still need to go to the potty station because they cannot go near the building or in the courtyard. Be sure your dogs are on a leash at all times. And wherever you go, please pick up your pet's potty."

"Johnny, if you were a dog, I'd get you some Depends panties so you wouldn't have to get out in the rain." The idea seems so funny to Eudocia that she breaks out in laughter and *thwacks* the handles of her wheelchair with her blue veined hands.

"Make sure you're picking up after your pets and returning the carts where they belong. This is an ongoing process and problem, and we are having to tell people to bring the carts back."

"What if I bring the cart back with my pet's potty-mess? In a bag? On the cart?" asks Eudocia wryly.

Don't leave trash on the carts. We have two push-carts with wheels at every elevator on each floor. Make sure if you use the carts you are cleaning up correctly and putting them back where they belong. If you dirty up the carts, please, please, please clean up after yourselves. Clean up the cart if you make a mess."

Lolly continues her spiel. She squeezes every breath through her nose, trying to imitate a friendly, upbeat tone, which gives her an unnaturally high pitch that suddenly drops on every downbeat. The more she talks, the flatter and more irksome her voice becomes. Lolly's words squirt from the ceiling with the force of an empty plastic mustard bottle being squeezed too hard.

In a fit of frustration, Eudocia suddenly grabs her jacket and umbrella from the hall closet. She spins her wheelchair around the corner and into the bathroom where Johnny's litter box is kept on the floor of the towel closet. She takes a grocery bag from the drawer.

"And have your dollar tip ready for the kitchen boy," says Lolly. "Don't make him stand at the door waiting for you to find a dollar. Be prepared."

"I'll give you a tip," Eudocia growls. "Get a new job."

Eudocia leans over and scoops litter and feces into the grocery bag, tying it tightly before rounding the corner again for the kitchen.

Also, the swimming pool, the theatre, the coffee shop, the craft room, and salon are still closed. We are, however, opening the library by appointment only, for one person at a time. You will have to wear a mask and gloves. And when you are in the clubhouse, remember social distancing. We still should be doing social distancing with everybody six feet away from each other."

"Bah humbug!" Eudocia snorts, grabbing her purse and keys from the kitchen counter. She tucks the grocery bag between her purse and one skinny hip. "Have I got a surprise for you!"

Remember, nobody on property, except essential people, like nurse's aides or people bringing you groceries. We know you miss your children and grandchildren, but NO children in your apartment! NO grandchildren in your apartment! They can stand outside your balcony and talk to you, okay?"

At this, Eudocia's face, which had been wrinkled up like an over-cooked sausage, begins to soften and sag. Her straight, pink lips pucker. Her natural scowl disappears, her mottled skin becoming soft as a coddled egg. She is thinking of her grandson, Thomas.

The image of her smiling grandson flashes through her mind, and from faraway she hears his child-like laughter. Eudocia wipes her eyes with the edge of her sleeve. She wonders if she will ever hug him again.

"Wear your masks when you're in the clubhouse, and really try to wear them everywhere you go…"

A familiar sharp pain squeezes Eudocia's chest. Her hands grow clammy. She sits perfectly still, waiting for the feelings to pass. Sensing something's wrong, Johnny rubs against her stockinged feet dangling from the wheelchair. She looks down and tries to focus on the blurry form of her cat.

"Not yet, Johnny," she whispers faintly. "I'm not goin' yet to the pearly gates."

Painfully, Eudocia navigates her wheelchair to the front door. She has been dreaming of her final act of rebellion for 64-days.

"Before I get my grilled Reuben, I still got one more job to do."

She rips the medical mask from the doorknob where it has been hanging since her last trip to the clubhouse. She pushes open the door. Slamming the *go* button on her wheelchair, she roars into the hallway, letting the door bang behind her without locking it. She sheers to the left and accelerates towards one of the four-wheeled carts sitting against the wall. She zooms forward at full-speed, reaching out for the plastic handle. Grabbing it tightly, she pulls the heavy cart alongside her wheelchair and smacks the button next to the elevator, which opens immediately. She hasn't moved so deftly since she last picked up her needlepoint.

Lolly's voice has followed her into the elevator. *"Remember social distancing…"*

Eudocia takes her gloves from her purse and inserts her fingers.

"This is what I think about social distancing."

She opens the bag of cat litter and methodically and carefully spreads the feces over the cart. She removes the soiled gloves and drops them on top of the mess.

"Don't forget to wear your mask."

"It ain't Halloween," Eudocia replies. With shaking fingers, she tries to tear the mask in half, finally using her teeth to gnaw through the thick paper before throwing it on the top of the feces and cat litter strewn across the top of the cart. By this time, she has reached the ground floor.

As the elevator doors open, the grayness of the interior hallway glumly greets her like a disheartened old man waiting to board, and a chilly breeze blasts inside, making her shiver. Eudocia's breathing comes faster, and her chest feels heavier. The adrenaline has disappeared, leaving behind weak and flabby arms. With great effort, she presses down on the *go* button. Overcome with tiredness, she glides through the shadowy interior hallway until she enters the long breezeway leading to the outdoor parking lot. From the intercom at the back of the elevator, she hears faintly Lolly's voice echoing, *"Have a blessed, Jesus-filled day…"*

Eudocia arrives at the opening to the parking lot and sits motionless in the cool outdoors. She looks up.

From the balconies, people are joyously ripping off their masks, throwing them to the wind. Like pale-blue flower petals, the torn pieces float in the air, some catching on the limbs of the pink-flowered crepe myrtles, swinging in the breeze like Chinese lanterns. The sidewalks are littered with their stretchy bands, curled and twisted like dead white snakes. The dark clouds with their full bellies of rain have scurried from the sky. And arching over the complex, she sees a pale rainbow.

A strange and powerful volition overcomes her. The desire to move. A mysterious force strengthens her, bidding her to rise from the wheelchair. With a sharp intake of breath, she stands.

As she leaves her wheelchair, she realizes that she is not alone. She is moving within a crowd of people, streaming from the apartment complex. Everyone is abandoning their masks and canes and walkers, drifting together towards the fields beyond the building, where the golden and lavender flowers grow, and the air is fresh and clean. Eudocia moves with them, rejoicing in the dawn of light.

Secret Life

They call her the Walker Woman.

She is an oddity among the other tenants who are young and flushed red-tan by the sun. She lumbers along, pushing her walker round and round the property, past the clubhouse and the pool, and up the road beside the grassy field.

When she's not bent over her walker, you'll see that she is a tall and skinny figure with fine-spun hair that sticks out everywhere. Her hair never moves in the prairie winds. It looks crispy-stiff as cotton candy sawing up out of a paper cone on a cold day at the carnival.

Walker Woman doesn't wear make-up. She doesn't care to slap blues and charcoals and pinks all over her face to satisfy your eyes—she doesn't care if you cannot reconcile the harsh contrast between her bile-colored skin and pink-white hair.

Her face and hands—the only parts poking out of her jacket—are made banana-spotted from the sun and age. Her skin appears no softer than a piece of old leather and her countenance no softer than the river rocks tumbled about the flower beds outside her apartment.

Mostly, she is a study in grays. She wears a dingy windbreaker over a T-shirt and faded silver-white jeans that she hitches up with an old plastic belt. In the right kind of light, she looks ethereally cloudy, from the dark circles under her eyes to the dirty shoes on her feet.

But inside, she doesn't feel gray.

Most can't see the little spark of breathless excitement that's lit up in the middle of her chest, but she feels it—feels it like a stelliferous kind of joy as wide as the sky and deeper than space—when she looks up at the stars.

Most nights you'll find her along the edge of the blacktop road, near the empty field with the for-sale sign in it. She's leaning on her walker, but her body curves like a rocket. She's arching upwards, waiting. Her head falls back, and her dark eyes have turned orchid-lavender, reflecting the bowl that holds the planets and stars, shaken upside down and spilling out all over her. In the glow and mystery, she is making wishes.

If the moon had eyes, it would see a face wrinkled by fifty years of smoking cigarettes—a face turned to pinches and creases and crevices. Like moon craters. If you happened to be driving by, you might see the flash of her lighter at the end of cupped hands. And your headlights would burst sudden-like on the silver, four-wheeled walker.

Her grown children will tell you that she refuses a motorized contraption. Too many moving parts, she says. Motors, and knobs and things that might break when you're in an inconvenient place, like along the side of the road at midnight. They'll also tell you that for entertainment—instead of getting a curly permanent hairdo at the beauty shop or playing Bingo with other old people—she smokes cigarettes.

In the early mornings, no matter what the weather, she leaves her apartment and pushes her walker down the road leading to the convenience store on the corner. She picks up a pack of cigarettes, a box of Twinkies, and serves herself a Styrofoam cup of black coffee. No sugar, she says. It's bad for you.

The clerk and everybody there know her by her real name. The delivery guy, Gary, is carrying in boxes of food and crates of sodas, stocking shelves with cans of Spaghettios and Vienna sausages and motor oil, when he sees her and says "Hi" and waves.

After breakfast and again around 3:00, she meets the couple in the van who park on the blacktop road. They call it their mobile smoking parlor because they live on a non-smoking property and the management will evict you if they catch you with a cigarette in your mouth. The white van is outfitted with a radio and a decent air-conditioner that keeps them from sweating through the hot summers.

When the weather is nice, they stand outside of the van and smoke and watch the traffic on the Loop, which runs parallel to the blacktop road, streaming past them on the other side of the grassy field with the for-sale sign.

They look at the livestock trucks carrying cattle for slaughter, and the mail trucks carrying packages, and the cars carrying people, and the school buses carrying kids. Walker Woman waves, hoping a child will smile and wave back. If they look up at all, they' don't wave. They stare, slack-jawed and vacant-eyed at the gray woman leaning on the walker with a cigarette in her mouth.

"Too many meds," says the mobile-smoking parlor man one day.

"Waddya mean?" asks Walker Woman.

"They keep 'em drugged up, those kids," says the man. "They's got sum kinder disease, or t'uther. That's why don' smile at ya when yer wave."

Walker Woman tastes the sweet, musky tobacco in her throat and blows it out slowly. She squints at the yellow school bus. She stares at it as it rolls away down the Loop. Moves away on purpose, going somewhere, anywhere but where she is. It disappears, and she doesn't say it or put it into words, but she feels that ache of loneliness that reminds her that it is disappearing like everything else in her life.

The only thing she could count on were the stars. Although they moved, too, depending on the seasons or the sky. But they always came back around, bright and predictable and smiling from the heavens upon the earth.

Her mother loved stars. She had wanted to name her daughter, Star, but changed her mind at the last minute and put Stella on the birth certificate. Stella Walker. After all, her mother said, it means "star."

When she was old enough, Stella got to stay up all night with her mother in the backyard and watch the night sky. Her mother had said, "If you wish upon the right one, your wish will come true."

Stella couldn't remember ever wishing to be old. She never had a dream of pushing a walker around a rundown apartment complex where nobody knows her real name, a noisy place where everybody laughs and calls her Walker Woman and casts pity-eyes upon her.

She thinks she must not have wished upon the right stars...

It is early Spring, and the night is cool. The school buses are parked, and only a few travelers race along the Loop.

Walker Woman is alone. She stands by the edge of the road, looking at the Big Dipper as it points to the Spring constellation of Leo. She is tracking the shapes with her eyes, counting the stars, and her lips are moving.

Even though her one-bedroom apartment is half a mile away, high up on the third floor overlooking the walls of the next apartment, she has the strange feeling that where she is right now, this is really home, somehow. Not the couch, as comfortably saggy as it is, or the swift goldfish in the bowl on the kitchen table, or the rabbit-ear TV crackling and fuzzy. None of it matters.

Even her cigarettes don't matter. She hasn't touched one since she began her vigil on this Spring night on the blacktop between the apartment complex and the convenience store, right at the edge of the field that sprouts weeds and grass intermingled.

And she is gazing up until her neck throbs with the agony-stretch, and her eyes are as watery as the sky.

She is remembering her mother's words: *"Stars are beautiful enough to break your heart."*

She feels something in her chest, or maybe it is her throat. A tight squeeze and then a release.

There it is, again.

She thinks, *I don't want to die with all the good wishes inside of me.*

She lets go of the walker. She lifts her hands slowly towards the luminous heavens. She takes shorter breaths. She smells the fresh-cut grass and dandelions and green weeds with tiny white flowers popping everywhere. She sees the blazing tail of a comet arcing towards the horizon, effulgent and bright, but to her eyes, hazy and dim.

She exhales. Inhales.

Feels the heavy fullness in her chest, rising and falling with every breath.

She thinks of her mother.

She remembers the prayer that her mother had taught her, *"If I die before I wake, I pray the Lord my soul to take—"*

She looks at the brightest star.

She fixes her eyes on it, determined to never let it go.

She wishes that her secret life would last...

forever.

Too Much TV, You'll Go Blind

The weather is weirder than a trailer park without any old people in it!" said Vince, peeking through the slats of the blinds in the living room.

Vince had never lived in a trailer park, but he knew a lot of old folks who did. And according to his wife, Peggy, he wasn't any spring chicken, himself.

"Nothing weirder than an old man standing at the window watching it rain," she answered from the kitchen. "Be thankful we live in a nice, new home and not in a tin can."

Lorna ignored Vince. She stood behind Peggy, hoping for another slice of roast beef. In the kitchen, dinner's leftovers had been stored neatly in Tupperware containers and placed in an orderly fashion in the fridge. Peggy made sure there was nothing left for Lorna to snatch.

"You're my little Cinderella," said Peggy, turning around to nudge Lorna into the living room. "But there's nothing for you to clean up tonight."

Lorna lumbered into the living room, and Peggy hobbled to the overstuffed, burgundy, easy chair where she lowered herself with a sigh. Lorna hefted her heavy frame onto the couch and stretched out luxuriously. Vince crossed from the living room's bay windows to the open and spacious kitchen, where he began scooping generous servings of chocolate Blue Bell ice cream into three bowls.

A bizarre outbreak of thunderstorms in January had kept Vince, Peggy, and Lorna inside their house for more than a week. On this particular Saturday evening, the downpour from a freakishly warm winter squall had passed through during the afternoon, dumping more rain. As temperatures soared through the day, and one storm built upon the other, the showers came in fits and starts.

"How 'bout a sugar overdose for my sweetie pies?" Vince asked. He carried a tray with the desserts into the living room, carefully placing each dish on the side tables next to Peggy and Lorna.

The ice-cream disappeared in a few slobbery bites as Lorna quickly devoured the contents of her bowl. She licked her lips with satisfaction and watched greedily as Vince and Peggy slurped the sweet drops slowly from their spoons. If not for muscle memory developed over seventy years, they would have missed their mouths because their eyes never wavered from the TV.

"Why aren't you on Channel 3?" asked Peggy. "It's almost time for the news." Vince and Peggy religiously watched Channel 3 news anchors Tim Terry and Karen Walker every night at 7 and 10.

"Hold your old bones," Vince said. "I'm on Channel 5 because Channel 3 News comes on right after Vanna's Wheel of Crap, which I prefer to miss."

A sudden crackling boom shimmied the house as a bolt of lightning struck a nearby cell phone tower. From a distance, thunder thrummed. Startled, Vince got up and walked briskly to the French doors leading to the patio. He examined the water-logged backyard, now eerily illuminated by the sickly greenish glow of the porch light.

"We may be ridin' out the storm in the attic," he said. "There's gotta be a foot of water out there right now, and more rain comin'."

"That nice Channel 3 weatherman will give us the forecast soon," said Peggy. "You know, I dated him back in high school." Her wrinkly face took on a dreamy, faraway expression.

"What? That squirt on Channel 3?" asked Vince. "What's his name? Winky Waterhose?"

Peggy ignored Vince and stared at the TV. A commercial for hearing aids blared.

"Vince, you need some of those. You've got terrible hearing."

Vince grunted and walked back to his La-Z-Boy recliner. "When you see a commercial for a new wife, let me know."

As the old grandfather clock on the wall chimed seven, Vince aimed the controller at the TV. The *tat-tat-tat* of the Channel 3 theme music rocketed into the room at higher decibels than the commercials. Suddenly, Tim Terry's square face filled the screen. His wavy brown toupee barely concealed the white curls of hair escaping from beneath it.

Lorna looked at her empty bowl with disgust. Tim Terry signaled the end of evening snacks until 10, and she was still hungry. She turned to gawk at the news anchor, imagining a hearty meal. The top of his head was mashed potatoes slathered with meat-colored gravy. She wondered if the puffy piece sticking up on the top tasted like roast beef.

"Stay tuned for Channel 3's exclusive reporting on today's shootings, arson, and impeachments," Tim said with a toothy grin. Behind his head flashed pictures of spinning police lights, burning buildings, and a bored congressman pounding a gavel on a table.

"Mayhem," said Vince. "The world's goin' to Hell in a handbasket."

"Global Warming," said Peggy. "It's making people crazy."

"Climate nonsense," snorted Vince.

After advertisements for laxatives and blood pressure medication, Tim Terry reappeared with his toupee firmly readjusted to hide the gray strands underneath.

"We interrupt our regular newscast for an urgent Channel 3 Storm Watch," he said.

The camera cut abruptly to an immense, rather dowdy-looking man wearing a silver suit and red tie matching his flushed face.

"Good evening, folks, I'm meteorologist Walter Sprinkler."

Peggy leaned forward with renewed interest. "Yes, yes, yes," she said enthusiastically. "That's him! My true love in high school. Winkie Boy!"

Vince let out a low whistle of surprise. "We've been watching the news together for five years, and you're just now telling me that you and that Sprinkler guy were a thing in high school?"

Peggy blushed. "I didn't want you to get jealous."

"It's kinda hard to be jealous of a guy who looks like that."

Nervous and uncomfortable, Walter Sprinkler pointed to a map behind him. A ring of sweat had drenched the collar of his dress shirt.

We've got a long night of storms, tornadoes, and flooding ahead of us. Keep it here for 3's Storm Watch."

Walter faded, replaced by an ad for flea and tick medication.

"See," said Peggy. "The weather is getting weirder."

"Not as weird as your weather boy, Winkie," said Vince, pushing off the armrests of his recliner to a standing position. Passing Lorna on his way to the kitchen he asked, "What do you think of the fat weather guy? Would you date him?"

Lorna blinked twice.

Peggy whipped her body around in her chair and opened her mouth to lob an insult at Vince, but he had already disappeared into the kitchen. That's when she noticed Lorna's claws.

"My, your nails are getting long, dear. Mama's taking you to get them trimmed and prettied up next week."

"Why do you call yourself *Mama*?" Vince shouted from behind the freezer door where he was rummaging for the carton of ice cream.

"That's what the doctor said when he brought her to us after she had that terrible surgery," answered Peggy. "He said, 'Here's your baby, Mama.'"

Lorna yawned. She needed another sugar fix to get through an evening of Channel 3 News. Vince slammed cupboards and rattled dishes in the dishwasher, searching for clean bowls. Finally, he shuffled back to the living room, carrying a super-sized bag of potato chips and a small bowl of chocolate ice cream.

"Here," he grumbled, putting the bowl on the table next to Lorna. "It's the last of the ice-cream. Don't say I never gave you nothin'."

Lorna felt the impulse to bite his hand, but the creamy cocoa swirl of sugary delight beckoned, and she resisted. Vince sat down in his chair and stuffed potato chips into his mouth while Lorna, mindful to keep her whiskers clean, delicately consumed her treat. Peggy goggled at the TV, enraptured by the female anchor who had joined Tim Terry. Peggy thought Karen Walker's perfect teeth were a marvel to behold, and her shiny face glowed with angelic beauty. Even her shimmering brown curls, quaffed into a sassy bob, mesmerized Peggy.

"Rain forced the annual citywide Pet Parade inside the Convention Center downtown, where hundreds of people crowded together to escape the storm and see the crowning of this year's winner," said Karen Walker.

"She could read the back of a box of bug killer and make it sound like poetry," said Vince with a sigh. "Wish I'd dated *her* in high school."

Images flashed on the screen of proud owners with prancing poodles. A slobbering Doberman dragged its owner across the stage at the end of its leash, and a shiatzu sat smartly in a tuxedo, pinned with a ribbon on his collar for first place.

"Wasn't Len's wife the winner of the Pet Parade last year?" asked Peggy.

"She's ugly enough to win," said Vince.

"No, I meant her labradoodle."

Vince turned up the volume. "Shh, your boyfriend's back."

The dreary-looking weatherman in a too-tight suit stood in front of a blue screen crawling with gigantic red and orange blotches. A massive red amoeba was inching its way towards the city where they lived.

"Folks, we're about to get slammed," said Walter Sprinkler.

At that moment, a gust of strong air swung the wind chimes outside. Lorna snapped upright and looked over her bowl at the French doors. Her body pulsed with the crackling white light that sketched the sky. Jagged sparks traced along the electric lines behind the house. Her skin tingled, and she thrust her head under a couch pillow.

"A Severe Thunderstorm Warning, Flood Warning, and Tornado Watch are in effect until midnight," said the meteorologist with a tremoring voice.

"Should we bring in the patio plants and furniture?" asked Vince nervously.

Peggy remained transfixed by the television.

"He's so handsome," she murmured. "Did you know, he once paid for half of my Dairy Queen meal after school?"

The pudgy weatherman pointed with a shaking hand to the red, orange, and purple blotches on the map, marching closer to their town. "Folks, you better have an escape plan."

"And to think that Winkie Boy almost took me to Homecoming, except he got strep throat," said Peggy. She had scooted to the edge of her chair, captivated by the meteorologist. "And to think he's now a famous weatherman…" she said breathlessly.

Lorna peeked from under the pillow. Peggy reminded her of a shriveled grasshopper stuck to the hot pavement on a sunny day. Very unappetizing. Shuddering, she turned away to study her empty bowl. Sometimes, a long, hard stare was enough to get Vince out of his chair.

Another sharp, sizzling crash of thunder shook the house. At that moment, a visceral desire for survival gripped Lorna. A primal fear urged her to make her own escape plan. Her appetite for a third bowl of Blue Bell couldn't hold her back. Leaping from the couch with an agility that belied her overweight condition, she ran pell-mell to the French doors. Her flight was so swift and silent that Peggy and Vince hadn't recognized the blur as Lorna. To them, it was nothing more than a stray floater that had suddenly appeared in their eyes.

Vince rose from his chair and stretched. The crinkling of the empty potato chip bag in his hands masked the popping sounds in his knees.

"Well, I'm gonna get the attic ready after I throw this away," he said. "Can't be too safe."

Hobbling to the kitchen, he caught sight of a big brown furball bumping her fat feline body against the doors leading to the patio. Vince rubbed his eyes. This wasn't a floater.

"Peggy, Mama—your baby wants to go out in the rain. Should I let her?"

Peggy's blurry blue eyes were stuck on Tim Terry. She watched with fascination as his potato and gravy hair slipped to one side of his head. The camera shifted to Walter, with his silver jacket fluttering like the rotating blades of a ceiling fan. Even his red tie had begun to flap violently, vibrating like a prop plane's propeller before take-off.

Vince pulled open the French doors which jerked violently backwards, banging against the wall as the pressure of two feet of water rushed into the living room. Gray and frothy waves crashed against Vince and Lorna, pushing them back. Lorna screamed and scrambled up Vince's leg. She balanced briefly on his shoulder, then wrapped her entire body around his neck.

"It's a flood!" yelled Vince, whacking at Lorna with one hand. "The dam broke!"

As he struggled to loosen Lorna's chokehold on his neck, he took steps towards the doors, reaching for the handles in a desperate effort to cut off the rising tide. Another enormous swell hurtled towards them, like the surf of the ocean as a hurricane approaches. Vince lost his balance, falling headlong into the deluge. Lorna's long claws served her well, hooking into the woolen collar of his sweater. She rode on his back as Vince floated face-down in the undercurrent.

As they were swept out the door, Vince managed to lift his head and spit out water. Gasping for air, he pummeled his arms back and forth. A burst of lightning revealed the live oak in the middle of the backyard, ghostly as the gray and white cardboard skeleton they had hung in their window during Halloween.

Swimming forward with Lorna glued to his back, Vince headed for the tree. The swirling surge propelled him until he could grab the thick trunk with both arms. Pulling himself to his feet, he hugged the tree like it was a life preserver. The wind chimes banged fiercely, their toll reminding him of an off-key requiem played by an organist at a funeral. Swinging back and forth from the collar of his sweater, Lorna clung desperately, hoping she would survive another day to eat ice cream.

Oblivious to the scene outside, Peggy sat comfortably in her easy chair, transfixed by what was happening inside the Channel 3 studios.

"I do believe he is going to lose his toupée!" she exclaimed.

A powerful torrent of water had blasted into the newsroom, ushered in by a violent cyclone that spun over the roof, tearing off chunks of tile and wood. As Tim Terry's hair blew off, the camera panned to Walter Sprinkler, who squatted on the top of his desk, crouching on all fours like a cat.

"This is a regular Noah's Ark kind of flood!" he shouted. "Better get your scuba gear."

"What a marvelous way to illustrate a weather forecast!" Peggy declared. "The visual effects are stunning!"

She hadn't noticed that her overstuffed recliner had been smoothly lifted by the rising waves and now floated easily like a purple barge. Her pink slippered feet were suspended above the gyrating waters, but her eyes never swerved from the TV. The large set remained immutable and cold, holding steadily on the table by the opposite wall.

An electric thunderburst illuminated the backyard, the heat and light crackling the top of the tree. Vince became rigid as the Halloween skeleton, plastered face-first against the live oak. Lorna's wet fur began to tingle. With precision and speed, she used her sharp back claws to dig deep into the warp and woof of Vince's sweater, climbing to his shoulders, springing to his head, and launching from his head into the thick branches, ascending until she found refuge.

The TV sparked and went silent, as the table rose buoyantly. The flood took the table, with the TV still atop. Peggy's easy chair had twisted in the same direction, following the table out the open French doors.

"Damn this remote," she muttered, aiming the controller at the blank screen as it bobbed past her.

Lorna caught sight of Peggy's gray head as she drifted beneath the tree.

"Winkie Boy, where are you?" she cried, frantically punching the buttons on the remote and cursing the TV.

The foaming floodwaters picked up speed, carrying Peggy in her easy chair past the tree and into the darkness beyond.

Lorna's green eyes never blinked.

SILLY SATIRE
The Power of Irony and Humor

Saint Ignatius of Loyola said, "Laugh and grow strong."

I admit I tend to be maudlin. The only cure for too much navel-gazing is a good laugh. Even better, I love to write stories that make others laugh. If you don't find the humor in these tales, you have my permission to use the pages to line your parakeet's bird cage. Perhaps, he'll be entertained by them.

Buffet to Die For

> *"The end of the human race will be that it will eventually die of civilization."*
>
> ~Ralph Waldo Emerson

Coffee Wars

> *"The second cup of coffee is never as good as the first."*
>
> ~Theodore Roosevelt

Cheese Whizz

> *"Boys, if you don't stick together, how do you expect me to follow you-ah?"*
>
> ~Lawrence Welk

BUFFET TO DIE FOR

I'll never forget the day June Goatby fell down dead in the parking lot of Duke's Diner. June was a bony, blue-haired lady who wore baggy print dresses and ran marathons in the Senior Olympics. Even though she was older than my grandma, she was healthy enough to have a live-in boyfriend. Nobody expected her to die while pulling up her pantyhose and laughing.

Her partner, Frank, had been out ahead of her, pushing his walker to the car after eating the all-you-can-eat Sunday buffet at Duke's Diner. He had said something so funny that she snorted and howled, slapping her knees and clapping her hands with uncontrolled merriment. That's when her tiny belly shook so hard that her pantyhose—which had hardly any elastic left because she was cheap and refused to buy new ones—snapped.

The tan stockings dribbled to her feet in a crumpled pile of sheer netting. Leaning over to retrieve them, she went into a nose-dive and crashed into the hot asphalt. There was no use reviving her. She had expired on impact.

I was lugging my tuba and music equipment inside Duke's Diner when it happened. I watched as a small crowd gathered around her lifeless body, which was face-down, stretched out like a stiff bedsheet, crinkled and rigid in the summer sun.

"Damn that meatloaf!" Frank shouted.

A group of middle-aged men with tattoos suddenly surrounded Frank. They pinned him against the driver's side door, pressing his walker into his stomach.

Frank began to whine.

"Well…you know…I mean…last week it was Eileen…that's

right, Eileen… getting sick from the…the…meatloaf, and now—"

The men grumbled with chins pointed up and fists raised. "You talk about our meatloaf like that, and we'll bash your Moo Goo Gai Pan you like so well!"

The baker, Indigo, peeked through the curtained window of Duke's Diner, then quickly returned to the kitchen to finish kneading a ball of dough. The other two chefs came outside and stood under the red and white awning. They scowled at Frank, sharpening their knives.

Duke Ham, the owner, swaggered out of the restaurant, moving past me with a car-salesman kind of smile, and positioned himself between the mob of Meatloaf Men and Frank.

"Skedaddle," he said. The men looked at Duke with stupid expressions.

Duke raised himself up to his full stature of five feet two and a half inches with boots on, and bellowed, "Go on. *Git!*"

The men turned away from Frank, as if snapped out of a weird mass delusion, and walked inside the restaurant. Meanwhile, the ambulance had arrived, and June Goatby was covered with a white sheet, placed on a gurney, and whisked away to Schmertz Funeral Parlor, where she was pronounced dead without benefit of an autopsy because the coroner said she was too old to need one.

Frank had slumped forward onto his walker, and Duke was now patting the top of Frank's head like he was a starved, homeless puppy.

"It'll be alright," Duke said soothingly. He pulled some crumpled papers out of his pocket. "Here. These'll git ya free Sunday buffets for a year." He snapped his fingers at the chefs. "Boys, bring him a sweet tea."

While the chefs hustled back inside to fetch a styrofoam cup of sugary Texas tea, I picked up my equipment and walked into the spacious, air-conditioned restaurant. Tuba players don't usually get gigs at diners, especially in small Texas towns, but Duke Ham was a different sort of guy who liked the sound of my sousaphone belching hit love songs. He gave me cash and a corner stage made of wooden crates where I played every weekend.

Later that night, while crooning on my tuba for a packed house, I kept thinking about June Goatby. For years, I'd heard the rumors about the food at Duke's making people sick. I never ate any of it, except for the garlic bread and yeast rolls. It was true that in the early '90s the menu had changed, and so had Duke. To top it off, he was becoming a tightwad. He wouldn't let me have my tip jar anymore.

I thought about June and how much she had loved eating the meatloaf. But she wasn't the first to eat it and die. Just two years earlier, Abby Applewood had keeled over at her table while consuming the beefy casserole with a side of garlic bread. Even though the coroner had said it was a heart attack, it seemed pretty suspicious to me considering the fact that Abby was in good health and not a day past 29.

Now, I'm just a musician, not some kind of Sherlock Holmes wannabe, but I decided right then and there that it was time for me to do a little sleuthing.

The next day, I walked around town asking my friends, nonchalant-like, what they really thought about Duke.

"He's lost his mind!" said Ben, the hardware store owner and one of the Meatloaf Men.

"How?" I asked.

"It all started when he got hold of some of those newfangled Ted Talks." Ben shook his head sadly as he rung up the box of nails I had purchased. "Yup, he's never been the same. He got cityfied. But his food sure is dang good!"

I stopped by Best Beauty Parlor for a pedicure. Floris, the beautician, clucked like a chicken when I asked her what she thought about Duke.

"His brain's addled by all that barbecue smoke!" she said bending over my big toe with an emery board. "Breathing in mesquite's jest as bad as smokin' cigars!"

She started chuckling as she filed my toenail. "But you know, I'm a Sugar Girl, myself, and I can't hep myself. I jest *luv* eatin' there."

A middle-aged woman with rollers in her hair pushed up the plastic bubble cover of the hair dryer and shouted, "Duke knows what he's doin'! He's gittin' ready ta run fer President, and by golly, I'd vote for 'im!"

I suppose, at this point I should slow down a bit and give you some background about me and Duke and the town. I was born and raised in Bliss, Texas. Nobody could remember a time when Duke's Diner hadn't been there. The two-story red brick building was a fixture on Main Street and had been built before the turn of the century by the first pioneers that set foot on that grassy field of cactus and mesquite. It wasn't long before the railroad rolled through bringing more people and business. Duke's great-grand-daddy by the same name brought his cowboy recipes, a skillet, and enough cash to rent the lower part of the red brick building. Over the years, it was obvious that Bliss was the perfect location for Duke's. It was the only town with a grocery store, bank, movie theater, and restaurant within thirty miles of three other farming communities. Granger, Bartlett, and Schmertz had mostly feed stores and grain silos. Plus, Bliss was one mile from FM 95, the back road to Austin, preferred by travelers avoiding the main highway.

Duke was a true Texan, who had left Bliss to spend his younger years driving cattle on the King Ranch in South Texas. When his father, the third Duke to run the diner, retired from the restaurant business, the younger Duke gave up the cowboy life and moved back to Bliss to continue the tradition. The younger Duke read Western novels and had a rifle hitched to the back of his pick-up. And he was a carnivore to the max. He served greasy cheeseburgers and spicy shrimp baskets every day of the week. Fridays were for fried catfish, and Sundays you could order up fork-tender barbecue brisket, smoked overnight on mesquite wood in the back shed.

Duke's was open late on the weekends. Farmers and their wives dressed in their best for dinner dates before catching a show at the Palace Theater down the street. The town's token Catholic family brought their ten children who made a cacophony of noise as the red-faced toddlers dribbled creamed corn down their chins and threw saltshakers at the waitresses. On Saturday nights, after high school football games, sweaty athletes and their bobby-socked dates would jostle at the jukebox, pumping in quarters.

When the jukebox broke, Duke hired me.

I played all the hits from the '60s and '70s on my tuba while a happy crowd chowed down. Everything was fine until a Houston entrepreneur opened an Italian restaurant next door. Happy Little Italy became the talk of Bliss. Weekends had people lining up outside the Italian restaurant's door, the line going all the way around the building and down the sidewalk, everybody willing to wait two hours for their spaghetti and meatballs and garlic bread.

That's when Duke hired an eighteen-year-old culinary school drop-out who had moved back to Bliss to live in his mother's basement. The kid had a knack for making five-layer lasagna, and steak and cheese manicotti, with unusual ingredients outlawed in Europe and Florida—things like red dye, artificial sweeteners, and monosodium glutamate.

To round out his Italian menu, Duke hired Indigo, the famous baker from Falfurrias, who had a reputation for making tasty garlic bread and cloverleaf rolls that were also unusual for their ingredients—whole-grain flour, water, salt, sugar, and yeast, put together masterfully with an old-fashioned technique that he had learned from his grandmother. The salt was extra special, because there were rumors that it came from an obscure convent in Ecuador where the nuns mined it from a secret cave. I don't know if that was true or not. But I sure loved Indigo's yeast rolls.

Duke opened up space for a dance floor, and asked me to start playing Italian love songs on my tuba. I learned songs like, "Un'Estate Italiana" which sounded better once I could afford to hire a vocalist and an accordion player. Before long, the lines went around the block for Duke's. The city slicker from Houston knew that he had met his match. Happy Little Italy shut its doors.

Like a sheriff in an old-fashioned Western movie, Duke strutted around town, flushed with the success of having driven the Houston entrepreneur out. He was proud of his popular diner, which was drawing customers from as far north as Waco, and even getting attention from the big city of Austin. Everything was going great, until the following summer—that's when a West Coast family showed up in Bliss and opened a Chinese restaurant next door to

Duke's. Jake's Panda Garden quickly became the new fetish, with its sweet and sour shrimp and egg-drop soup and a glass aquarium with a Komodo dragon.

Not to be outdone, Duke hired another culinary school drop-out, a kid who could whip up the best Moo Goo Gai Pan and Kung Pao chicken east of San Francisco, with enough MSG to, "choke a mule," as Duke would say. But Duke didn't stop there.

He bought an enormous commercial-grade silver buffet that stretched from one end of the restaurant to the other. There were giant metal pans overflowing with Italian and Chinese, plus the favorites everybody had loved before—greasy cheeseburgers and spicy shrimp baskets. There was also pepperoni pizza, corn on the cob, thin-sliced honey ham, pickled okra, steamed broccoli, and cupcakes. An entire section had been designated vegetarian with fruit salads, greens, and meatless meatloaf. Indigo baked tray after tray of fresh garlic bread and cloverleaf rolls, while the chefs sizzled, fried, and boiled their way to gastronomic stardom.

Even after the West Coast family shut down Jake's Panda Garden, Duke continued to transform the image of his restaurant, improving the décor and the menu.

He made sure that the chefs added generous amounts of vegetable oils, artificial sweeteners, red dye—anything to make the food richer and more colorful and, as Duke would say, "flavorsome." The food appealed to the eye. Ribs were dyed mahogany, and glistened with a slathering of Crisco. Mac and cheese glowed neon orange. Duke added Scottish Haggis and Turkish Khash and Tuna Eyeballs from Japan.

The changes in the menu were part of his "personal transformation," he said. Nobody could quite figure out what had happened to him—his cowboy nature had changed, and his carnivore appetite had changed, too. He ate more salads and wore pink button-down shirts with his jeans. He donated his Western paperbacks to the library, and walked through town throwing around weird sayings and slogans, but with a Texas accent. He called his menu, "Fried and Diversified," and his diner, "The Buffet to Die For."

Duke's Diner went beyond being a *comfort food* place for old farmers and their wives. The fame of his food spread, and his restaurant soon became an attraction for tourists heading up north by the backroads and winter Texans driving south. It was a favorite hang-out for weary truck-drivers and a secret pleasure for musicians and hippies who considered it weirder—and tastier—than anything in Austin. It made the Triple A *Bucket List of Restaurants to Eat at Before you Die*. The Governor of Texas signed a proclamation declaring the month of August, *Duke's Tolerance and Diversity in Food Month*. A food critic from the *Austin American Statesmen* wrote a glowing piece about the place, saying:

"Duke Ham, A Texas cowboy at heart, is refreshingly open-minded about the cosmic evolution of food. Every menu is stamped with the motto, 'Don't Hate—Appreciate.' Ham's fearless inclusivity of radical ingredients has inspired an enviable unity among disparate groups, bringing together vegetarians and carnivores, vegans and butter-lovers. Truly, there are no walls or borders at Duke's Diner."

That was true, in the beginning. There was a hearty acceptance of every dish, and everyone jovially tolerated one-another's differences in taste. It wasn't uncommon to see plates piled high with diverse pairings like cheeseburgers and tofu lettuce wraps, or vegan tofurky dogs on gluten-free bread alongside Bratwurst dripping with butter. But over time, people became obsessed with the food they loved most, and began forming little clubs. There were the Ghost Pepper People, the Butter Bunch, the Meatloaf Men, the Moo Goo Gai Pan Club, and the Sugar Girls. They were obsessed with their dishes. Addicted.

Every once in a while, somebody would get sick after eating at Duke's Diner, but nobody wanted to blame their favorite food. Duke liked to joke that it was "edgy food."

Frank called it "edge of death food. Eat the meatloaf and you'll die!" he declared after June passed away face-down on the pavement.

Everybody laughed at Frank. Duke called him "a conspiracy theorist." After all, Duke said, nobody had died from eating at his diner. At least there wasn't any cause-and-effect kind of correlation. Even the four doctors in the town ate the food, and one of them had retired and now lived in Gonzalez. The other three died prematurely of stomach cancer, but nobody could prove their stomach cancer had been caused by eating at Duke's.

A few weeks after June Goatby died, I decided that it was time to do a little sleuthing and ask the question—Did the meatloaf really kill the little old lady with the blue hair?

"So," I said in a round-about, relaxed way as I stood behind Gary, the plumber, who was on his hands and knees, fixing my toilet, "wasn't it strange that June Goatby died after eating the meatloaf at Duke's?"

Gary put down his wrench and looked up at me. "You know, I think it's them Sugar Girls," he said. "I'll bet you my bottom dollar they were spiking June's iced tea with artificial sweeteners, and you know that causes cancer."

Later that night at the monthly Bingo game at the Baptist Church, I shared Gary's accusation with the Sugar Girls, a group of elderly ladies who devoured anything sweet and fattening. They were shocked. They claimed that the Ghost Pepper People had dropped a handful of jalapenos on top of June's meatloaf, and "That's what killed her!"

Saturday night, between song sets, I chatted with the Ghost Pepper People, who expressed outrage by the insinuations of the Sugar Girls. They protested that they were being targeted for a crime they hadn't committed. None of them had died. Yet.

The rumors percolated for a few days, but then everybody went back to business as usual. I continued playing my tuba on the weekends and eating Indigo's bread with generous dollops of butter. Even if the meatloaf hadn't killed June, I wasn't going to tempt fate by eating it.

Then, just six months after June Goatby had dropped on the parking lot, Tom the mailman and his wife Sophie got sick after eating at Duke's Diner. Tom had eaten the meatloaf, but he blamed it on the enchiladas, even though he hadn't put any on his plate. Sophie had been eating her favorite Italian dish, steak and cheese manicotti, but she blamed her stomachache on the fresh fruit salad that nobody had ever seen her go near, let alone eat. After that, the Vegetarian Club vowed to boycott Duke's for all eternity.

Duke took to social media to clear his name. He threw around slogans, like, "Bein' Anti-Food ain't No Good." He spouted studies of red dye and artificial sweeteners that proved these combined ingredients increased mitochondrial efficiency in WWII soldiers, accounting for all of their winning battles. He became a Twitter icon, doxing anybody who disagreed.

He passed out coupons for free Sunday buffets, added a free ice cream cone dispenser for the kids, and gave everybody free lemon meringue pie on their birthdays. He took out ads on the radio and boosted posts on Facebook. It wasn't long before business picked up again, and profits soared. Duke must have been feeling generous because he gave me back my tip jar.

The next summer rolled around, but I hadn't quenched my curiosity about June Goatby. While it was still cool enough to drive my pick-up with the windows down, I decided to take a road trip to Gonzalez, where Bliss' 95-year-old doctor, Jose Hernandez, had retired. We met in the sunny lobby of the nursing home where he lived, and I told him the whole story.

"So, is it the meatloaf?" I asked.

"Maybe," he answered. "June was in good health. Abby was young. The other three doctors, esta loco! Crazy, as you would say. All of them dying of stomach cancer. But did they eat the meatloaf?"

"The doctors loved the Chinese and Italian," I said.

"So, it's hard to determine which food could have been the culprit," he said. "All of it has unusual, even slightly toxic ingredients, in varying amounts. But nothing is outlawed, except in Europe and Florida."

"It can't be the bread," I said, "I love those rolls."

"Does the bread have copious amounts of unusual ingredients in it?"

"Nope," I said. "I think it's just water, flour, and yeast. Oh, and some kind of special salt. Indigo says it comes from some obscure convent in Ecuador."

"Hmm…I've heard of that. The nuns mine the salt from a secret cave and have it blessed, right?"

"That's what I've heard."

"Did June, Abby, and those three doctors eat the bread?"

"Everybody eats the bread," I said. "It's the best."

"Ahhh...."

He leaned back against the chair. He was quiet for a long time, thinking. Then he spoke in a strange voice. He seemed to be in a trance, his eyes glazed and his tone deep and serious.

"*They crave what kills them,*" he said in a slow drawl.

"What?" I asked.

"*...and it kills them slowly...*"

I felt like I had entered the Twilight Zone. "What kills them slowly?"

"*Everything,*" he answered.

"Everything?" I shouted. I couldn't believe that I had just wasted a tank of gas to find out that everything at Duke's Diner would kill you.

"No, no, no—" he whispered. Then he leaned forward with a serious expression on his face and grabbed my hand with his bony fingers. "*Everything except the bread,*" he said.

"We've got to call the authorities!" I yelled. "We've got to shut it down!"

Jose shook his head and fell back on his chair.

"It doesn't happen all at once," he said. "And it's hard to prove. But I'll tell you what killed June and Abby and those doctors. It's eating all that other food, with its minute amounts of impurities and toxins—it's enough to kill them slowly, over time. But then, they eat that simple, plain, pure and beautiful and blessed bread..."

His eyes suddenly blazed with an angry fire.

"It hastens their death!" he said firmly. "*They can't eat both and live!*"

He slumped in his chair, exhausted.

I thanked the doctor and drove back to Bliss, breaking the speed limit and almost hitting an armadillo crossing the highway and twice running red lights. I was lucky there weren't any cops around. I pulled up in front of Duke's Diner and ran crazily into the kitchen and found Indigo, kneading a ball of dough. I pulled him towards the meat locker, and whispered what I had heard from the doctor. Then, I begged him to leave town.

"Why not tell *them* to change their food?" he asked, nodding at the two culinary school dropouts chopping tomatoes nearby. "It's their ingredients making people sick. My bread has nothing bad in it!"

I had to admit that eating Indigo's bread was the best thing I'd ever done. My acne had cleared up, my allergies gone away, and I never got constipated anymore.

"That's the thing," I whispered hoarsely, "these people want to eat what's killing them! They're addicted. Besides, Duke would never fire *them*."

I jerked my head towards the two chefs.

Indigo's face turned hard and determined. He returned to the kneading bowl and began punching the dough with a zeal I'd never seen.

The summer passed, and even though nobody else had died, I was a nervous mess every weekend, worrying about Indigo's bread.

In the meantime, Frank, who'd been alone since June had died, found a new girlfriend named Opal. One Sunday afternoon, he took her to Duke's Diner for a date.

He strictly warned her to avoid the meatloaf. She happily agreed, and they ate platters of Moo Goo Gai Pan with a side of Indigo's fresh yeast rolls. While I was playing my tuba, I saw them eating the yeast rolls, and almost had a panic attack. Even though the air-conditioning blasted icy puffs from the vents above my head, I sweated until my clothes stuck to my body, and the wave of hair on my forehead was limp as a noodle.

When they got up to pay for their meal with the coupon that Duke had given Frank for Sunday buffets, I quickly finished my song, put down my tuba, and hurried to the front door, where I watched them as they walked to the car.

I heard Opal make a joke that was slightly sexy about the backside of Frank. He looked at her in surprise, and when she winked at him, he began to laugh so uproariously that he choked on the noodle between his teeth, the one he had been poking at with a toothpick. With one final guffaw he lost his grip on the handle of his walker and pitched forward towards the pavement, the walker rolling away as he dropped to the ground, "deader than a doornail," as Duke would say.

A small crowd came out of the restaurant and gathered around his motionless body. There was no use reviving him. He had expired on impact.

"Damn that Moo Goo Gai Pan!" Indigo shouted.

The baker had run out of the kitchen when he heard the commotion outside, pushing past me and into the middle of the parking lot where he stood next to Frank's lifeless body.

A group of Millennials with piercings suddenly surrounded Indigo.

"Hey!" they growled in unison, pinning him to a nearby car. "Don't bash our Moo Goo Gai Pan like that, or we'll dis your bread!"

"The food…" Indigo cried, "It's making you all crazy!"

Opal fainted. A few of the Sugar Girls who worked out on Saturdays at the local gym grabbed her before she hit the pavement, and dragged her inside the restaurant. That's when Duke swaggered out with a car-salesman-kind-of-smile and positioned himself between the Moo Goo Gai Pan Club and Indigo.

"Everything we serve at Duke's Diner is FDA approved," he said. "Besides, everybody loves the food that our chefs make."

The two chefs, who had come to the doorway, smiled smugly. Duke began weaving through the horde of people, passing out coupons for free Sunday buffets.

Everyone roared, "Duke's Diner's finer!" and, "Damn the rest, Duke's the best!"

Even the policeman and the medic who had arrived began singing, "So delish, you can't resist!"

Now, I don't know exactly who started it, or where it came from, but somebody threw a garlic baguette at Indigo. That's when there was a rush to grab entire baskets of rolls from inside, which became crusty little bombs in the hands of the people.

Everybody yelled, "Indigo's bread makes you dead!"

Indigo covered his head with his hands, ducked low, and ran madly down Main Street, chased by the Meatloaf Men, who pelted him with the hard bread until they all disappeared around the corner.

In the parking lot, the crowd began to cheer for Duke, and threw their sunglasses and hats into the air. The Millennials put Duke on their shoulders and carried him, while everybody danced and pranced like it was a holiday along Main Street.

I went back back inside and picked up my tuba gear from the stage and quickly walked down the sidewalk, away from the diner. I had barely made it to the end of the street when I heard Duke's voice, carrying strong and clear on the smoky, mesquite-filled air.

"Free sweet tea for everyone!" he yelled, as the people cheered and the ambulance drove slowly past me, taking Frank's body to the morgue.

That was the last day that I ever played love songs on my tuba at Duke's Diner. I had enough money in my tip jar to buy a ticket on the next morning's train to Florida. I sat down on the blue-cushioned seat beside a man who was reading the local Bliss newspaper. I noticed the headline on the front page read, "Duke's Diner Wins Customer Satisfaction Survey for the 100th Year in a Row."

The man put the newspaper in his lap and shook his head with disgust. I recognized his wrinkled face and slicked-back hair. It was Indigo.

"What are you doing on the train?" I asked with surprise.

"Going to Florida, starting a bakery. No more buffets."

"Oh," I said, patting my music case sitting beside me in the aisle. "Need a tuba player?"

Coffee Wars

George was the self-proclaimed java genius in the house, making miserable anyone who dared to resist his dinosaur ways. His wife, Tess, had surrendered to his coffee mastery long ago. Their son, Frederick, had not.

It was Christmas break, and Frederick had come home from college, bringing a bag of Tanzania Peaberry and his glass-blown Chemex. The first morning, Frederick scooped the mahogany grounds into a natural filter that he had tucked into the Chemex' concave mouth. He boiled water in the tea kettle and poured the slightest bit through the Chemex, waiting for the coffee to bloom. In ten minutes, he slowly dispensed more.

Gravity gradually pulled the water through the coarsely-ground beans and into the bell-shaped glass, producing a fragrant infusion, frothy, dark, and smooth. After drinking one cup, Frederick stored the rest in a large mason jar that he kept in his parents' refrigerator. His father, George, condemned the practice one morning.

"You don't need to drink three-day old coffee from a jar," he snarled, tossing it in the trash. "We've got this new Mr. Coffee."

George lovingly patted the top of its black plastic cover. "Isn't it beautiful? The coffee-making wonder of the world."

Frederick grunted. "Mine's in the Museum of Modern Art," he said, slouching over his mug of steaming Tanzania Peaberry spiked with crema and cinnamon.

From across the kitchen, they heard a shattering. Tess stood over the sink, her chin drooping to her breastbone, her shoulders rolled forward in defeat. Frederick jumped up and sprinted to her side. Looking in the sink, he saw the broken pieces of his Chemex.

"I was washing it, and it slipped," she whimpered.

Frederick's eyelids began to twitch. George's pale lips spread upwards, pulling his sagging skin into bulging knots beneath his eyes that sparkled with devilish delight.

"You're in my coffee world now, boy," he said, chuckling. George grabbed a bleached filter and a can of Folgers from the cabinet.

"One-hundred percent Arabica," he said authoritatively. "Four scoops. Four cups of purified water. Pour carefully. Flip the switch."

The machine sputtered and steamed. Frederick thought the potion dripping into the pot looked like black sludge.

"What if I don't like it?" Frederick asked, frowning.

"You'll like it," George said. "Don't use your crap in my Mr. Coffee, okay?"

Frederick grimaced. The thought of staying all week in his parent's house without his Chemex seemed worse than downgrading from an iPhone to an Android. He knew his father's coffee impositions had to be endured, because George was footing the college bills.

The next morning, Frederick dutifully followed his father's instructions. After the pot had brewed, he sat down at the kitchen table with a mug. Even with cream and sugar it tasted bitter.

An hour later, George shuffled into the kitchen in his bathrobe and emptied what was left of the carafe into his cup. He choked and spit it into the sink.

"That's cold!" he shouted. "The machine's shut off! Didn't you know it turns off automatically after thirty minutes?"

Frederick shook his head. "No."

"After you make it, turn it off manually," George said emphatically, clicking the switch down. "Then turn it back on." George pushed the switch up again. "That way it's still hot when I get up."

The next day, Frederick did what his father had asked. When George walked into the kitchen, the pot was still hot. He poured a cup and took a sip. Disgusted, he threw it in the trash.

"That's old," said George. "It's been sitting too long. It isn't fresh. In the mornings, dump yours and make it new for me, okay?"

Saturday came, and Frederick searched everywhere for George's plastic red Folgers container. Finally, he gave up, and drove to Starbucks for a carton of coffee. When he got back to the house, he put it into the Mr. Coffee and flipped the switch.

His father stumbled into the kitchen and picked up the steaming pot of coffee, and filled a mug to the brim.

"What the hell is this?" George gasped, sputtering and red-faced after taking a gulp.

"It's Liquid Energy," said Frederick. "Single sourced. From the mother country."

"Speak English, boy."

"It's Starbucks. I couldn't find yours."

George leaned over and pulled the plastic red container from under the sink. He shoved it at Frederick, who caught it and fell backwards into his chair.

"I told you not to use your crap in my Mr. Coffee!" shouted George.

"Yours is crap" yelled Frederick. "You don't know where the hell those beans came from!"

"I get those beans from the same place every time," George said. "Piggly Wiggly."

George turned his head and stared at the coffee maker.

"Is my Mr. Coffee leaking?" he asked.

"No," said Frederick.

"Why's all this water here?" asked George, looking at the countertop.

"Maybe I spilled some," said Frederick.

"You need to wear your glasses when you make coffee."

The next morning, Frederick obediently made two rounds of coffee exactly as George wanted. As the coffee maker finished percolating, George lumbered into the room in his bathrobe and filled his cup with the black brew. He sat down beside Frederick who was sitting beside Tess while they ate scrambled eggs and bacon. George swallowed gingerly. His lips puckered. "For a college boy, you sure don't know how to make coffee," he said disapprovingly.

When the day arrived for Frederick to leave, he decided to be reckless. He would unashamedly display the evidence of his sloppy, generous, modern coffee ways.

Using one of his natural filters in the Mr. Coffee, he added five scoops of Tanzania Peaberry, and haphazardly poured an entire pot of purified water through the bin, watching it splash everywhere. He smiled, satisfied that he had won the final skirmish with his father.

After drinking three cups, Frederick packed his bags and left the house feeling slightly jittery and quite triumphant.

Yawning, George stumbled into the kitchen and prepared a cup of coffee with powdered creamer and a packet of Sweet'N Low. A few minutes later, Tess walked in to find George on his knees with his hands raised.

"Amazing," he exclaimed in worshipful awe, holding the coffee pot in the air like it was a sacrifice to the coffee-gods.

"What?" asked Tess.

"Frederick finally made the perfect cup of coffee."

Cheese Whizz

We named our band Cheese Whizz to avoid copyright issues. Also, because we all agreed the product in the jar with only one z—not two—was our favorite condiment, ever. The girls put it in their enchiladas. George and Frederick loved to heat it up in the microwave until it got that brown, crusty ring around the top of the jar, and then they'd dip tortilla chips in the gooey orange mess. And me? I liked to pour it generously over mac and cheese. It's a dish to die for.

Cheese Whizz had a flush of success for a few short months at Indigo's bakery in Tally—short for Tallahassee. But the genesis of it all was me and my sousaphone. At first, it was just me and my tuba, playing '70s hit love songs on the weekends.

Then, Indigo started getting requests for jazz. Pretty tough to play solo on a tuba. I was thinking about pinning up a "help wanted" sign at the local music store when the gals came in for donuts. There was just something about them that made me think they could sing.

"Are you gals singers?" I asked.

They smiled and nodded, and launched into a rousing rendition of Sinatra's "Fly Me to the Moon," in five-part harmony, which is no easy thing for three singers. They were older than my grandma, but I didn't care. They had the voices of angels.

But the most important question I had was this:

"Do you like Cheez Whiz?"

Stella pushed her walker against the wall. Then, she put her gigantic purse on the table and took out a huge casserole dish steaming with enchiladas.

"Take a bite," she said, handing me a fork.

I scooped a large piece from the pan and crammed it into my mouth. There was a happy explosion of Cheeze Whiz when I bit the middle.

"Excellent," I said. "You're hired."

So, there we were. Me and the three gals, Eudocia, Stella, and Peggy, the Cheese Whizz Band.

"I can't sing on Fridays," said Peggy. "I have TAA."

What's TAA?" I asked.

"TV-aholoics Anonymous," she said.

Indigo booked us on Saturday nights. I played cool jazz, and they crooned to the oldies at Indigo's bakery. Mostly we played for croissant-eating medics getting off work and truck drivers drinking coffee to stay awake. We were pretty good, but not good enough to draw a crowd. We needed a guitar and drums.

It was Eudocia who found our guitarist and drummer. One night around ten, two men walked in. The father and son ordered coffee and donuts. The father loved the old-fashioned sour cream donuts and the son preferred a chocolate éclair.

When they sat down at the table, the father took a sip of coffee and yelled, "What the hell is this?"

The son smiled and said, "It's your favorite, dad. Folgers."

I watched Eudocia walk over to the table. She had been miraculously healed of leg problems and had given up her wheelchair years ago. She said that's when she discovered music.

"Do you boys play any instruments?" she asked.

"I play guitar," said the father.

"I play drums," said the son.

Then, she asked the most important question of all.

"Do you like Cheez Whiz?"

Frederick pulled a jar out of his oversized coat pocket.

"Got some chips?"

George laughed and pulled a supersized bag of tortilla chips from inside his oversized jacket.

"Got a microwave?"

That's how George and Frederick became our guitarist and drummer.

I suppose I should have asked if they were any good at their instruments, but at the time, that didn't matter. Lucky for us, their rhythm and skill almost matched the beauty of my mac and cheese with extra Cheez Whiz.

Our first gig on a Saturday night at Indigo's Bakery we attracted a small audience. They were there mainly for the donuts, I know, and most of the patrons were on their cell phones. But a few watched and even clapped their hands between bites of their cinnamon bear claws.

They must have liked us enough to come back and bring their friends—or maybe it was because of Indigo's flyers at the public library. The next weekend the crowd doubled in size. What was really incredible was that most people didn't even look at their cell phones. If they did, they were recording us and uploading the video to Facebook.

The tip jar went up from five bucks to twenty-five bucks.

We were on a roll. A drum roll. We were better than free cinnamon rolls.

The crowds expanded every Saturday night. Word got out about the jazz band, Cheese Whizz at Indigo's Bakery.

The last weekend we ever played there, the bakery was jam-packed with customers who stayed for the whole set. They stood shoulder to shoulder, singing along to the jazz hits we played. They stuffed the tip jar with bills. They built a mock-up of a Grammy award with glazed donuts and presented it to us before the encore. But we knew we were better than a jar of Cheez Whiz when they put their lighters in the air and waved their Danishes to "Ain't' Misbehavin'."

It brought tears to my eyes.

The band's success was a happy accident. Kind of like ordering a glazed donut and getting one with chocolate frosting and Bavarian cream inside, instead.

Fame is fickle, though. The starving musicians suddenly got hungry for more. When the tip jar went up from twenty-five bucks to $3,000, that's when the trouble began.

"We should get most of that," complained the three ladies.

"We bring years of experience. We could die any day. It's battle pay!"

"No, no, no," growled George. "We're the heart of this Whizz group! If it weren't for me and Frederick here, you wouldn't have a beat or a rhythm."

"Hey, what about me?" I said. "I founded this group!"

We argued all night and into the morning until finally I agreed to split all the money between the trio of ladies and the father and son.

"You're all fired," I said after paying them. "Take your jars of cheese substitute and go home."

"This was gonna be my last weekend, anyway," said Peggy. "I'm getting out of town for a while. The weatherman says a hurricane's brewing in the Gulf."

I'd like to say that we stayed reasonably hostile to each other, like all good musicians usually do after a band break-up. But we didn't. We send each other Christmas cards and new and interesting recipes for Cheez Whiz.

George has us over to his house every once in a while. He's a fierce competitor when it comes to Crazy Eights and Old Maid. He's also a coffee guru, too, with the best java I've ever had. Frederick drops by during the holidays when he's on break from college. And every once in a while, the trio of old gals gets us together for Twinkies and a jazz singalong. As they've gotten older, they've developed a unique six-part harmony.

Indigo occasionally joins us for cards and snacks, bringing a batch of his famous yeast rolls. We never eat them with our Twinkies. Definitely not with Cheez Whiz. Stella claims the crusty, sweet little breads make her feel like dancing. She's even put up her walker and started jogging.

Sometimes, we talk about the good old days of Cheese Whizz.

Success was sweet, even if short.

We miss the packed house and the thrill of crooning the oldies under the strobe light that Indigo put in. But I'll take success the size of a bag of donut holes over a contentious argument over a tip jar, any day.

And I think we all agree that we get along better, now that

it's just me and my tuba at Indigo's playing '60s and '70s hit love songs.

ACKNOWLEDGEMENTS

To a super publisher, Mike Parker, who believed in my author dreams, and had the publishing wisdom to make them come true.

To Keb and Tina, my writerly sisters, who stuck with me for the three years it took to finish these stories, and whose keen eyes and editorial sensibilities saved them from storytelling faux pas and grammatical doom.

ABOUT THE AUTHOR
KIRA MARIE MCCULLOUGH

Kira Marie McCullough is an award-winning author of short stories, debuting her first book with WordCrafts Press. Her short stories have earned awards and applause. "Buffet to Die For" became a finalist in the Tennessee Williams Literary Festival Contest, 2020. In 2019, "Her Best Kiss" was performed before a live audience in New York City as part of Liar's League NYC's "Short & Sweet Flash Fiction" event. In 2014, she received the "Creative Writing Award for Fiction" from Texas A&M University-Central Texas. Several other short stories have been published in online journals and magazines over the past decade.

Follow Kira online at:

https://kira-marie-mccullough.com